$1.90

Joe Haldeman lives in Iowa and fought in the Vietnam
War after gradu... ...from
the University o...

He is rapidly bec... ...science
fiction, and mos... ...el,
THE FOREVER WAR, which won the 1976 Nebula
Award, will also win the much-respected Hugo Award.

Also by Joe Haldeman

THE FOREVER WAR

Joe Haldeman

Mindbridge

Futura Publications Limited
An Orbit Book

An Orbit Book

First published in Great Britain 1977
by Futura Publications Limited
Copyright © Joe Haldeman 1977

ISBN 0 8600 7932 5

Printed in Great Britain by
C. Nicholls & Company Ltd
The Philips Park Press, Manchester

Futura Publications Limited,
110 Warner Road, Camberwell,
London S.E.5.

Contents

1
Blessed Are the Peacemakers

Denver pissed him off.

Jacque Lefavre had managed a long weekend pass from the Academy, and at the last minute decided to go to Denver instead of Aspen. It looked like rain.

Indeed it rained in Denver, bucket after cold bucket, time off at midnight for sleet. In Aspen, he learned later, it had been eight inches of good powder snow.

He went to the Denver Mint and it was closed. So was the museum; government holiday. He went to a bad movie.

He was walking along with his overcoat open and a cab splashed him from collar to cuff. Traveling light, he'd brought no other outer clothes.

The hotel's one-hour dry cleaning service took twenty hours. They wouldn't admit they'd lost the trousers.

He drank too much room-service booze, sitting in his room watching daytime TV in his underwear.

When he got his uniform back, they had neglected to roll the cuffs. He would have to re-iron them when he got back to Colorado Springs.

The desk clerk would allow him neither student discount nor military discount. He had to shout his way all the way to the assistant manager, and then they only gave him the reduced rate to get rid of him.

The train broke down and was six hours late.

He stomped his way through the sleeping dormitory, in mild trouble for coming in after curfew, and smelled fresh paint when the elevator stopped at his floor.

His roommate had painted their room flat black. Walls,

ceiling, even the windows. Jacque had painted the room at the beginning of the semester, to cover up the government green. Now he discovered a curious thing.

There was a limit to rage.

"Uh, Clark," he said mildly. "What, you didn't like beige?"

Clark Franklin, his roommate, was stretched out on the bed, chewing a toothpick and studying the ceiling. "Nope."

"Personally, I thought it was rather soothing." He felt deadly calm but abstractly realized that his fingernails were hurting his palms. He stood at the foot of Franklin's bed.

Franklin shifted, crossing his ankles. He hadn't looked at Jacque yet. *"Chacun à son goot."*

" *'Goût.'* I don't like the black very much."

"Well."

"You should have asked me first. We could have arrived at a compromise. I would've helped you paint it."

"You weren't here. I had to paint it while I had the time free." He looked at Jacque, lids half closed. "The beige was distracting. I couldn't study."

"You lazy son of a bitch, I've never seen you crack a book!" A neighbor thumped the wall and shouted for them to keep it down in there.

Franklin took the toothpick out of his mouth and inspected it. "Well, yeah. Couldn't study in the beige."

The next morning the registration clerk told Jacque he would have to wait until next semester to get a new roommate. Four months.

Actually, Franklin moved out a few weeks early. He left three teeth behind.

2
Autobiography 2062

I've never used a voice typer before but I know the general idea you've got to damn you've got to press the character button and say period. . . . There. Comma , , , , It works, how about that. Paragraph button now.

My name is Jacque, spelling light comes on, Jacque Lefavre. If it were a French machine it probably would have spelled out "Jacques" and the hell with it, but no, that's right the way it is up there, without the final ess.

This is for the archives, I mean ARCHIVES damn. Got to touch the capitals button then get off it before you say the word. Starting over.

This is for the Archives of the Agency for Extraterrestrial Development. Motivational analysis and training evaluation survey. Highly confidential, so get your eyes back where they belong.

Begin at the beginning, my freshman composition teacher used to say, and I could never figure out whether that was profound or stupid. But all right, the beginning. I was conceived sometime in the spring of 2024. We'll skip the next eighteen years or so.

But I should say something about my father because that is important. And if what they say is true, that this won't be read (spelling light again, crazy language) for another twenty years, then people will probably have forgotten who he was.

My dad's—Robert Lefavre's—shining hour was the paper he delivered at the 2034 American Physical Society meeting. It was called "The Levant-Meyer Translation: Physics as Wishful Thinking." Look it up, it's very convincing. It was well-received. But the next month, Meyer sent a mouse and a camera to Krüger

60 and they came back alive and full of exposed film, respectively. Via the LMT.

So in one day my father was reduced from Nobel candidate to footnote.

Even as young as I was, I could see that something broke in my father when that happened. Something snapped. With hindsight, now, I have sympathy for him. But he was a ruined man, and I grew up disillusioned with him, contemptuous and hostile.

It's kind of a kick, watching this machine spell. I couldn't spell contemptuous if my life depended on it. Now if they could only program it to put the semicolons in where they belong . . .

So as far as motivational analysis, I guess the main reason I became a Tamer was to hurt my dad.

After his anti-LMT thesis was demonstrated to be wrong, Dad took a sabbatical from the Institut Fermi and never went back. Maybe they asked him not to return, but I doubt it. I think it was just that he would have had to start work on applications of the Levant-Meyer Translation, like everyone else at the Institut. After spending six years trying to prove that there was no such thing as the LMT; that the freak accident that happened to Dr. Levant had nothing to do with matter transmission, but could be explained in terms of conventional thermodynamics.

So we gave up the nice Manhattan brownstone and moved upstate, away from Institut Fermi and the weekly seminar at Columbia, to a little junior college where Dad became one-third of the physics department.

He hated the job, but it gave him plenty of time outside of class. He would stay locked in his study all morning and evening, oblivious to us, trying to find where his thermodynamic proof had gone wrong. Mother left in less than a year, and I left as soon as I was old enough to take the Tamer examination.

My nineteenth birthday came just three days after I graduated from gymnasium (we'd moved back to Switzerland in

2042), and that morning I was the first one in line at the AED employment office in downtown Geneva. The testing took two days, and of course I passed.

I went home and told Dad that I'd been accepted, and he forbade it. Those were the last words he ever said to me. I didn't even see his face again until his funeral, nine years later.

Dad's attitude was the familiar one (then), that we had just come too far, too fast. Less than a century had gone by between the first unmanned satellite and interstellar travel via the LMT. We hadn't even finished cleaning up after the Industrial Revolution, he claimed—and here we were planning to export the mess to the rest of the Galaxy. And war and et cetera. We should grow up first, put a moratorium on the LMT until the race was philosophically mature enough to handle the vast opportunity.

Who was going to tell us when we'd grown up enough, he didn't say. People like him, presumably.

So I slammed the door on his silence and went on to the AED Academy in Colorado Springs.

(Reading over the above, I can see that it gives a pretty lopsided picture of my motives for joining the AED. Although my father's extreme stance in the opposite camp was very important, especially in keeping me from quitting the Academy when it got rough, I probably would have tried to join no matter what my family situation was. The profession seemed romantic and interesting, and my generation had grown up coveting it.)

I'm not the best Tamer to ask about "training evaluation." It took me six years to get through the Academy (in those days a lot of people got through in four), even though I had no trouble with the course work or the physical training. My semester reports were always marked "profiled for psych."

They've loosened up on this a bit, over the years. But when I was at the Academy there was one quality they valued over all others, for the people who made up a Tamer team: icy self-control. The kind of person who would face certain death with a slightly raised eyebrow.

They never got perfection, because they also were looking for qualities such as imagination and resilience, rarely found in robots. But I did have to admit that all of my fellow students seemed rather more self-possessed than I was. Mainly, I had one hell of a time controlling my temper. They put me through psychoanalysis and situational therapy and even made me study Buddhism and Taoism. But then they would test me with the damnedest things, and I would always flunk and get profiled.

They liked to use ringers, for instance. I got a new roommate once who turned out to have been an actor, and who spent a whole semester perfecting his role. He would borrow things and never return them, express outrageous opinions without deigning to argue about them, contemptuously refuse to study and yet get high grades. Plus a whole galaxy of small annoyances. And then, in the middle of the study week preceding the semester's final exams, he sauntered into the room and announced that he had won over my current lover. And he had revealed to her certain things. Things a man will tell another man and feel protected by bond of gender.

I hoped the AED repaired his nose and fixed that kneecap. I left him there bleeding and went out to walk through the snow, actually afraid I would kill him if I stayed in the room. I stomped around until my fingers turned blue, then returned to find him gone, replaced by a note from my psych counselor.

It turns out that the two extra years served me well later on. I took a heavy load of technical electives, and things like discrete tectonics and atmosphere kinematics came in handy when we got down to practical geoformy. With a broad, general knowledge of the physical and biological sciences, I've always drawn more than my share of trailbreaker assignments. The first Tamer team that goes to a planet has to have a couple of generalists aboard, to help decide what sort of specialists will go on subsequent trips. And it's a lot more fun to crawl around an unexplored planet than it is to go in with pick and shovel and geoform it. For me, anyhow.

Studying oriental philosophies didn't improve me the way the psych board hoped. But Taoism did save my ass in a very direct way, in what I later learned was my final, make-or-break, situational exam. It also involved an actor.

My Taoism instructor was a kindly old gentleman named Wu, full of humor and patience. I was headed for Germany on summer break, and not planning to do any serious studying, but out of respect for him I agreed to continue the *I Ching* readings. Even though I privately considered the book's wisdom to be only slightly more profound than the little notes you get inside of fortune cookies.

So every morning I would compose myself with contemplation and prayer, trying not to feel silly, and then ask the *I Ching* a general question about the day ahead of me. Then I'd toss the coins, look up the proper commentary, and commit it to memory, so I could refer to it at various times during the day.

I don't even remember the question I asked that morning before my final testing. But I'll never forget the commentary:

> Here a strong man is presupposed. It is true he does not fit in with his environment, inasmuch as he is too brusque and pays too little attention to form. But he is upright in character, he meets with (proper) response . . .

It struck me as oddly appropriate, and all day I walked around trying to be not-brusque and proper. That night, as I had done every night since coming to Heidelberg, I went to a quiet, inexpensive bar down the block from my hotel to read and relax from the day's sightseeing.

A bellicose drunk was abusing the bartender for not serving him. I watched the argmuent for a while, noted privately that the big fellow could use a dose of the *I Ching* more than another drink, and returned to my reading.

I looked up when the argument stopped, and in the mirror behind the bar caught a glimpse of the drunk lurching by behind me. Then for no reason he picked up an empty stein and tried with all his might to brain me with it.

I didn't know it at the time, but the AED was not going to allow me a seventh year of training. They didn't care whether I got my brains bashed out for inattention or stopped the assault by simply punching the guy. Or breaking his back; he was getting paid enough to compensate for a long hospital stay or a prison term for second-degree murder.

Either way, I would have flunked out.

But I saw it coming and grabbed his wrist and twisted the stein away from him. I set it on the bar and asked him, "Do I know you?" in pretty good German, in a low voice. When he responded with a stream of bilingual invective, I told the bartender to call a cop. The "drunk" left.

The anger, bitter anger, hit me a few minutes later, in trembles and cold sweats and grinding teeth. But instead of going off in a rage, finding the guy and pulverizing him, I remembered who I was trying to be, and kept it bottled up. And wound up spending the rest of the short evening on my knees in the john.

There were three other people in the bar, and one of them was an AED observer. The next day, I got my papers.

3
Personnel Report

Satellit Übersendung Mitteilung ITT

ZU John Thomas Riley Director of Personnel AED Academy Kabel Adresse: STARSEED	VON Hermann Kranz Abraordnate für Mann schaften AED München Deutschland	RECHNUNG- NUMMER 01 285 7H496 «Kollekt'	DATTEL 29 Juli 5	ZEIT 02.10

My Dear Riley:

As directed, I was present at the informal testing of Tamer
Candidate Jacque Lefavre. I am trying to reach you by telephone, but
get no response from your office or home. You must be in the early
evening, it is 2.00 AM here.

It is my pleasure to report that Candidate Lefavre ~~acted~~ reacted with
dignity and restraint. He was obviously very angered by the encoun
ter, but contained his anger even when the effort made him physically
ill.

I was reading on the train to Heidelberg your profile of
Candidate Lefavre and had myself developed quite a "case of nerves."
I was certain that here tonight I would see, one man or the other,
murdered. But I think that, in your analysis, that Candidate
Lefavre would perform much better under extreme stress than he
does in a classroom situation, you were completely correct.

A tape of the confrontation was made from a ceiling camera,
and will ~~will~~ be forwarded to your office along with my complete
report. When you see it, I think you will agree with my evaluation,
that Herr Lefavre deserves no less than a 1.00 stress response rating.

I spoke to Herr Lefavre at the bar, before the actor began his
job. His German is bad even for a Swiss. But he seems to be a personable
young fellow, and I look forward to meeting him under less artificial
circumstances.

Suzanne and I will be in Colorado next month, and we look very
much forward to calling on you.

Cordially

Kranz

4
Roster

GROOMBRIDGE 1618 MISSION, 17 AUGUST 2051

PERSONNEL:
1. TAMER 4 TANIA JEEVES. FEMALE, 31.
   8TH MISSION. SUPERVISOR.
2. TAMER 1 HSI CH'ING. MALE, 23. FIRST MISSION.
3. TAMER 1 VIVIAN HERRICK. FEMALE, 23. FIRST
   MISSION.
4. TAMER 1 JACQUE LEFAVRE. MALE, 25. FIRST
   MISSION.
5. TAMER 1 CAROL WACHAL. FEMALE, 24. FIRST
   MISSION.

EQUIPMENT:
5 GENERAL-PURPOSE EXPLORATION MODULES W/
STANDARD EQUIPMENT
1 PERSONNEL RECORDER
1 HOMING FLOATER (SECOND SHOT)

POWER REQUIREMENT:
2 SHOTS 7.49756783002 SU, TUNING @ LOCAL TIME
13:21:47.94099BDK477
13:27:32.08386BDK477

MISSION PRIORITY 5.

FUNDING #733089 TRAINING.

5
Chapter One

Jacque Lefavre's first world was to be the second planet out from Groombridge 1618. It wasn't an especially promising place; the planets accompanying small stars rarely pan out. They wouldn't have wasted an experienced team on it.

Tania Jeeves was helping Jacque adjust his suit's biometric readout. "Ten to one it's just a rock. A hot rock or a cold one, we'll see."

The five of them were standing around the Colorado Springs ready room, having a last cup of coffee while putting their suits through final checks. They would be living in the suits for the next eight days.

"You don't think we'll find anything interesting, then?" Carol Wachal said. "Just an expensive training exercise?"

"Well, it's always interesting. No two are alike, not even the rocks."

"But you don't think we'll find any life?" Jacque said.

Tania shrugged and snapped shut the lid of the readout box. "I wouldn't expect a Howard Johnson's. Maybe fossils, maybe some tough species like the Martian nodules."

A door at the other end of the room opened and a technician looked in. "Ten minutes," he said. "Right after the next incoming." The door led to the staging area, where their suits would be sterilized. Once clean, they would go on to the vacuum chamber that held the LMT crystal.

"Time to zip up," Tania said. She pulled the tunic up over her head and tossed it into a locker. The others did the same.

Jacque noticed that Ch'ing discreetly avoided looking directly at his female teammates. Jacque himself lacked that particular grace, but at least had the politeness to examine each woman with equal interest. Carol returned his stare and added a deadpan wink.

All five were in excellent physical condition and attractive in spite of their hairlessness and rather overdeveloped muscles. Tania had faint stretch marks from having given birth six times on three different planets, and hairline cosmetic surgery scars under each breast. But they were marks of her profession and didn't detract from her beauty.

Out of reflex vanity, Jacque stood in such a way that the women couldn't see his back. It looked as if someone had kept score on it—with an axe. Twelve years before, he had been chased down an alley and pinned to the ground by four men while a fifth tried to find his kidneys with a straight razor. This was evidently done for amusement, as they already had his wallet. He and his father moved back to Europe as soon as he got out of the hospital.

The suit, or "general-purpose exploration module," was a roughly man-shaped machine that could keep a hardy person alive for as long as a month in the middle of a blast furnace or swaddled in liquid hydrogen. Inside it, one could stomp through a hurricane without being blown over, walk the ocean floor without being crushed, or pick up a kitten without hurting it.

It had several tools that weren't obviously weapons. With them and with the help of the suit's strength-amplification circuitry, one could: make a pretzel out of a steel bar; reduce a city to rubble; run around the equator of a small world in a week. But it took you five minutes of contortions to scratch your nose, and certain other parts of the anatomy were simply inaccessible.

You learned to live with it.

The suits were damned expensive and rather difficult to operate. Simpler attire was available for worlds where the conditions were known ahead of time. But it was profitable to outfit a planet's first Tamer team this way, since the only alternative was to send an unmanned probe ahead first. And the biggest expense in any Levant-Meyer Translation was energy, which was the same whether you were transporting a fully outfitted team or a small probe. Or a rusty beer can, for that matter.

Someone who was body-modest or squeamish could never learn to get along with a GPEM suit. You became too intimately a part of it; it recycled everything. Fortunately, those who got past all the tests and training to finally become Tamers couldn't possibly be squeamish. And modesty was unlikely to be a strong force in their character.

Fitting yourself into the rigid suit was an operation similar to what a medieval knight had to go through to get into his armor. From a waist-high platform you lowered yourself into the bottom half. While your arms are still free, you hooked up the abdominal and femoral sensors and relief channels. Then a crane lowered the top half of the suit over you while you held your arms up, so that they slid easily into the suit's arms. (Which was the reason for the difficulty in scratching your nose. There was just enough room inside the suit to twist and turn and manage to get one hand free without dislocating your shoulder. But it took time and determination.) An automatic locking mechanism sealed the top half to the bottom. With your tongue and chin you turned on the suit's radio and optical circuits . . . and you were ready to go.

Jacque clicked on his radio. "I've never been in one of these things for a week," he said. "It must get pretty ripe after a few days."

"Some people, yes," Tania said. "It's all in your head."

That's right, Jacque thought, my nose is in my head. He experimented with the image amplifier, tonguing it from infrared to ultraviolet and back. It didn't make much difference in the indirectly lit room; the pastel colors just washed out and came back.

"Well," Ch'ing said. "Shall we—"

The door swung open and four suited figures came into the room, moving easily in their tonne-weight suits. Just returned from God-knows-where, their suits had a coating of pale blue dust. A thrill moved up Jacque's back and set his scalp prickling, a feeling he had subdued for the past six years, knowing that not one candidate in twenty actually made Tamer 1.

He was going off the earth. Even if it turned out to be just an airless slab of cold granite, it was a place that no human had ever seen before.

"Let's go." They followed Tania into the sterilizing room, a cubicle with mirrors for walls, floor, and ceiling. Every half meter there was a slender ultraviolet-to-gamma tube. "Keep well spread apart. At least a meter between your outstretched arm and the next person."

The reflections of the five people bounced back and forth, multiplying them into a vast army that stretched to the horizon in every direction. The door sealed and a pump throbbed somewhere, sucking air out of the chamber.

"Turn off your eyes." The feeling of being in the middle of a huge crowd was replaced by claustrophobia: sealed inside a roomy coffin. Jesus, Jacque thought, how long could you stay sane if your opticals failed?

"Okay." They turned their eyes back on and followed her to the LMT chamber. Two technicians on the other side of a window watched them file in. The light from the window was the only light in the room, but it was adequate to show them the way to the crystal. "Four minutes, ten seconds."

The crystal was a glass gray circle, 120 centimeters in diameter. Tania stepped just over the edge of it.

"Carol, you can be on the bottom with me. Ch'ing and Vivian next, then Jacque on top." Here any similarity between the GPEM suits and old-style armor vanished. Tania and Carol stood face to face in the middle of the circle while the next two climbed up to stand on their shoulders. Then Jacque clambered over all of them to be King of the Mountain. The gyroscopic stabilizers that ringed their suits' waists kept the fragile pyramid from collapsing.

A glowing yellow cylinder of translucent plastic slid down

over them. This was just a guide to keep them inside the LMT field; they were safe so long as they stayed a couple of centimeters from the plastic. Anything not inside the field when the current pulse came would simply be left behind. It didn't have to be an arm or a leg; just a little piece of the suit would be more than enough.

"Ninety seconds." Nobody said anything. "Thirty seconds."

"Hot or cold?" Vivian said. "Any bets?"

"Bet you a dollar it'll be just like Earth," Carol said. "But you'll have to give me a thousand to one. Ten thousand."

"Yeah," Jacque said. "Biosphere must be thin as an eggshe—"

6
Biospheres: Classroom 2041

SCENE: Classroom in an exclusive, old-fashioned private school in upstate New York. Drowsy hot day in late spring, airco broken.

CAST OF CHARACTERS: TEACHER is William J. Gilbert, M.A., this form's instructor in the physical sciences. He is annoyed at the class's lack of attention but thinks he has hit upon a device that will liven things up. JACQUE LEFAVRE did not do the previous night's homework and doesn't know a biosphere from a bowling ball. Two days before, he has officially dropped the terminal "S" from his name (because he was tired of being called "zhocks") and, instead of taking notes, he is practicing his new signature. Assorted STUDENTS and one FLY.

TEACHER

Sitting on the desk—trying not to seem stiff.

> I think that the text's explanation of the biosphere is rather obscure.

Gets off the desk, stiffly.

> Do you agree, Mary?

FIRST STUDENT

Yes, sir. But I think I understood it.

SECOND STUDENT

Whispers to THIRD STUDENT:

> Jesus, what a brown-nose.

TEACHER

Did you have something to say, Ronald?

SECOND STUDENT
No, sir. Just that I think I understood it, too.

Class reacts predictably.

TEACHER
You have no idea how happy that makes me.
Reaches in drawer and brings out a navel orange.
Perhaps a demonstration will make it equally clear to everybody.
Produces pocket knife and opens it with a flourish.
How many people have had calculus and analytic geometry?
Only three hands go up as he carefully cuts through the skin and rind, making a circle around the middle of the orange.
Very well, then. I won't call this a locus.
He twists and worries at the orange until he has three pieces: the fruit and two hemispheres. He sets the fruit aside.
These two halves of the skin and rind will be our biosphere model.
He puts the two hemispheres together.
Imagine, if you will, that there is a tiny star in the center of this sphere.
He sets down one half and points to the inside of the other with a pencil.
Since the star is in the center, any point on this rind is going to be the same distance from the star. Thus, every point on the rind will get the same amount of energy from the star, and will be at the same temperature.
Taps the outside.
Likewise with the skin. Same distance all around, same temperature. A little cooler than the inside.

FOURTH STUDENT
Inverse square law.

TEACHER

Very good, Stan. But please don't interrupt.

A FLY has entered the room and is buzzing very loudly, trying to escape through the windowscreen. The TEACHER glances at it for a moment, then continues.

TEACHER

We will say that the temperature of the inside of the rind is a hundred degrees Centigrade, the boiling point of water. The outside skin is where the temperature is zero degrees, the freezing point.

Now, Mary. Will you tell the class what that means?

FIRST STUDENT

Quickly

It means that the only place in the system where you can have liquid water is the volume that corresponds to the rind of the orange.

TEACHER

Very good. What else?

FIRST STUDENT

After a moment:

Everywhere else you'll just have steam and ice?

TEACHER

Looks at the FLY again but decides not to go after it.

That's true, but it's not exactly what I'm looking for. Anybody else? Mark?

FOURTH STUDENT

Puts down hand.

Where there's no liquid water, you can't have life as we know it. Because carbon-based life . . . needs water . . .

TEACHER

—as a more-or-less universal solvent, that's right. And

that's why we call it the *biosphere*. *Bios* is Greek for life, and only in this *sphere* can life exist. Amy?

FIFTH STUDENT

But last year in Biology Miz Harkness said that a biosphere was all the air and water and . . . ground on Earth, where plants and animals can live.

TEACHER

Gruffly:

A word can have more than one meaning.

The FLY stops buzzing and JACQUE looks over at it. JACQUE has been trying to look inconspicuous, but it's difficult because he's the largest one in the room, and the vagaries of the alphabet have put him in the front row.

TEACHER

Jacque? Could I have your attention?

JACQUE

Yes sir.

JACQUE has lived in America for eleven years and has no trace of a French accent. When he returns to Switzerland in nine months, with a slowly healing back, he will have lost forever the musical Lausanne accent that surrounded him as a child, and will speak his native tongue like an educated foreigner.

TEACHER

Bearing in mind what Mary and Mark just said, tell me: which would have the larger biosphere, our sun, or a hot blue star like Rigel?

JACQUE

Hesitates.

Our sun?

TEACHER

Absolutely not! The lesson last night used Rigel as an example. Didn't you study it?

JACQUE

Uh . . . sir . . . we had a . . . voltage fluctuation last night and I couldn't get the book to work.

TEACHER

Shakes his head

I wish I had a dollar for every time . . .

Rhythmically slapping his palm with a ruler.

Your assignment for tonight, then, Jacque, will be to write a four-page paper about the biosphere. In it you will explain why one is more likely to find a hospitable planet going around a hot star than around a relatively cool one.

JACQUE

Yes, sir.

TEACHER

And you will read it for the class tomorrow. And answer questions.

The voltage fluctuation story is true. Even at this age, JACQUE knows more about physics and astronomy than the TEACHER does. William Gilbert's M.A. was in Music Education. When he reads his paper tomorrow, JACQUE will point out that by the TEACHER's definition, the Earth is not within the Sun's biosphere [since if Earth were airless; the temperature on the surface could exceed the boiling point of water, as it does on the moon], and therefore cannot support life. He will also remark that the extent of Rigel's biosphere is meaningless, since young blue stars don't form planets. Thus he will make a powerful enemy, not for the first time or the last, and would be destined to flunk the course if the alley rendezvous were not to cut short his semester.

Chapter Two

"—eggshell."

Like some improbable circus act, the Tamer team suddenly appeared less than a meter above the surface of Groombridge 1618's second planet. They fell abruptly, and found that the planet did indeed have liquid water. More to the point, liquid mud.

"Jesus Christ!"

"*Merde!*" Jacque fell the farthest and so sank the deepest, up to his shoulders.

"Hold it," Tania ordered. "Nobody move for a second. See whether we keep sinking, whether it's like quicksand."

"I don't think it is," Jacque said. "Think my feet are on solid ground."

"Try to walk, then."

"No problem." Walking, Jacque made a gelatinous sucking sound, and the black mud swirled viscously behind him. "Uh, heading toward that bush. Or whatever it is."

The planet, which they would simply call Groombridge, was within its star's biosphere and obviously had a primitive form of plant life. Not green, though. Jacque was headed for an organism that did have a recognizable stalk and drooping fleshy plates that might be called leaves. But it was the color of a corpse.

Groombridge 1618 hung high in the sky, easily four times as big as the sun is from earth, but looking unwell. It was a dull orange color, mottled with black spots and etched with fine swirls of yellow faculae. Its brightness was tempered by the dense low fog, and one could look directly at it without squinting.

The pale yellow fog limited their visibility to some 70 meters; half again that far in the infrared. At the extreme limit they could barely make out what might have been the edge of a forest. Or at least a group of largish plants.

"It's a . . . a good planet." There was a trace of wonder in Tania's voice. She wasn't looking at the dreary landscape, but at the information that appeared projected in ghost images onto her viewplate:

GRAVITY	0.916	ARGON	0.028
TEMPERATURE	27.67°	METHANE	0.004
ATMOSPHERE:		XENON	0.003
PRESSURE	0.894%	SULFUR OXIDES	10E-7
NITROGEN	0.357	CARBON MONOXIDE	10E-7
ARGON	0.297	NITROGEN OXIDES	10E-8
OXYGEN	0.212	HYDROGEN SULFIDE	10E-8
WATER VAPOR	0.051	AMMONIA	—
CARBON DIOXIDE	0.047	HALOGENS	—

This didn't mean they could open their helmets and start breathing. For one thing, there was too much water vapor and carbon dioxide: sitting still in a chair, you would start to pant in a few minutes. And there were things like bacteria, viruses, and nerve gases that a suit's equipment couldn't detect, but which could be fatal in concentrations of less than one part per million.

But Tamers had brought more formidable worlds under control. Groombridge might never be the garden spot of the universe, but if the AED thought it worth the trouble, men might walk unprotected on its surface in not too many years.

"Wish we'd brought a mouse," Carol said.

"Next time. We'll take some air back."

8
Geoformy I

(From *Sermons from Science* by Theodore Lasky, copyright © 2071, Broome Syndicate. Reprinted from *The Washington Post-Times-Herald-Star-News*, 16 September 2071:)

"To geoform" is a transitive verb, an inelegant neologism that means, rather obviously, "to change into [something having certain qualities of] earth."

The first planet to be geoformed was earth itself.

Consider: men can't destroy a planet's ecology, not with hydrogen bombs, not with nonreturnable bottles (remember them?). All they can do is change it. Even a featureless radio-active billiard ball of a planet has an ecology, albeit not a complex one.

Men started to geoform the earth in the middle of the twentieth century. Unfortunately, a lot of the early work was done by people who failed to see the earth as a closed set of mutually interrelated systems. Typically, they would drive around in petroleum-powered vehicles, picking up cans (which were trying their damnedest to rust and get back into the soil). Then they'd drive the cans to a recycling place that ultimately burned coal to melt down the cans to make more cans. In the process they were using up very finite supplies of fossil fuels—and incidentally gave New Jersey the most spectacular sunsets this side of the planet Jupiter.

More generally, the problem was that in order to fix something up, you have to apply energy to it. And taking energy from anywhere on the earth—be it coal, uranium, or a waterfall—will have an effect on the earth's ecology. So you have to fix that up, too. And so on.

The obvious solution was to get energy from someplace else. The sun wastes 99.999% of its energy trying to warm empty space.

23

So in the fullness of time, they tossed up a couple of satellites with huge mirrors that turned sunlight into electricity. The electricity powered big lasers, also in orbit, that pumped energy down to ground-based collectors. From that point on, things got complicated, but suffice it to say that there eventually was plenty of extremely cheap energy which could be had at no expense to the environment.

They made the deserts bloom. Unfortunately, nature is perverse in this regard, and making one desert bloom will turn some perfectly good piece of real estate somewhere else into a new desert. What the hell, send up another satellite. It took quite a few satellites, but eventually the whole world was covered with green grass and nodding grain and the sweetest air this side of the Garden of Eden.

That this organic, polyunsaturated paradise was precariously maintained by the several million megawatts of brute power that streamed down from the sky every second—this was only the concern of a handful of scientists and technicians who smoked too much and snapped at their spouses.

Eleven billion people lived fairly comfortable lives because of those megawatts. But theorists estimated that if the power failed, fewer than one in ten would live out the year. And it was unlikely that the survivors would be very civilized.

It looked as if geoformy might provide a kind of insurance against this rather probable disaster: make an alternate earth, an independent colony on another planet. Then humanity could go on even if earth were in a shambles.

To this end they did a limited kind of geoformy on the moon, roofing over the crater Aristarchus and filling it up with air, water, crops, and farm animals. But it was too expensive a project to maintain, and so was abandoned after a few years.

Mankind might have lived on forever—however long that turned out to be—in this state of artificially maintained grace, and never geoformed any planet but Earth. But forty years ago today our universe changed, because of a random lightning bolt that struck a research building in the suburbs of College Park, Maryland. . . .

9
The Levant-Meyer Translation

(From *Science for Everyman* by Russel Groenke, Hartmen TFX, Chicago, 2059. Copyright © Hartmen House, 2059. R28, C10:)

The Levant-Meyer Translation is named after two American scientists, the one who accidentally discovered the process and the one who refined it into a practical device for interstellar travel.

Many scientific discoveries have come about accidentally. For instance, one of the times the element phosphorus was discovered, it was because an alchemist's cook had forgotten to take dinner off the fire (see R12, C39). And Galvani's dinner of frog legs—that twitched when touched by two different kinds of metal—led to the invention of the storage battery (see R21, C53).

The accident that happened to Tobias J. Levant was not culinary in nature, but literally a bolt from the blue. In his own words:

I had set up an experiment with a large (about two centimeters across) crystal of calcium bromide. Calcium bromide is an "ionic conductor," and so conducts electricity only at relatively high temperatures.

The purpose of the experiment was to record changes in the lattice structure of the crystal as it was heated, with a small electric current going from one face to the opposite. A special kind of electron microscope was trained on the crystal.

There was a violent thunderstorm that night, and the

laboratory lights had flickered several times, but I decided to go ahead with the experiment. The only part of the setup that was on line current was the small heating coil that encircled the crystal, which was not critical. The laboratory had an emergency generator that would go on automatically if the power failed.

A freak discharge of lightning struck the wall of the laboratory (ignoring the lightning rod on the roof) and a brilliant blue arc enveloped the heating coil, simultaneously with the thunderclap. The lights went out and there was a strong smell of burning insulation. I felt a sharp pain in my finger but had obviously been neither burnt nor electrocuted.

The lights came back on in another part of the laboratory—the wiring had been vaporized on my side—and I went over there to call the fire department. Once in the light, I could see that the tip of my forefinger had been sheared off. So I called a doctor as well.

I was a little stupid from shock and got the idea that I ought to go back into the laboratory—before it burned down—and find the end of my finger, so it could be sewn back on. I found a lantern and made my way through the smoke, back to my bench.

The heating coil was just a charred mess, but oddly enough the crystal itself seemed unharmed, glittering like a lens where it had fallen on the tabletop.

When the lightning struck, I had been adjusting the controls of the electron microscope, so I looked for my fingertip there. I didn't find it, but did see an amazing sight.

A hole had been bored straight through the machine, in line with the axis of the crystal and exactly the shape of the crystal's cross-section. At first I thought the lightning bolt had burnt through, but there was no charring or melt. That part of the electron microscope had simply ceased to exist.

It reappeared seconds later, in midair, directly over where the crystal lay, and fell with a great clatter. Pieces of metal, electronic components, and my fingertip, all in a jumble over the tabletop.

With my good hand I retrieved the fingertip. It was frozen solid; so cold that it stuck to my skin and left a burn. The metal objects had become rimmed with frost and were smoking—a kind of cold I had never seen outside of a cryogenics experiment.

While the firemen were tearing down the wall to get to the smoldering insulation, I was calling every scientist and engineer whom I knew well enough to drag away from dinner. We met in lantern-light around the shambles of the electron microscope.

That very evening, Theo Meyer came up with what turned out to be the correct explanation. While the doctor was tending to my wound, he said, "Tobias, you've invented a matter transmitter. Your finger just went to Jupiter and back.

(*—Time* TFX, 16 Oct 2034, Copyright © Time Inc., 2034)

It had gone considerably farther than Jupiter, of course. As Meyer himself was to find out, the minimum distance an object can be transported by the LMT is on the order of 10^{14} kilometers, or about three parsecs. We'll never know exactly where Tobias Levant's fingertip went, but it was deep space.

It took several minutes for Jacque to force his way onto solid ground, or at least relatively solid mud. The bush he had followed for a reference mark was the only vegetation around; there was nothing nearby resembling grass or moss or even algae. From his vantage point he could see that the "forest" yonder was simply a clump of bushes slightly larger than his own bush.

"Time for the floater," Carol said. They had been on the planet seven minutes.

"Depends." The floater had been launched a little over five minutes after the Tamer team. It was somewhere on the planet, probably in the same hemisphere. But it was impossible to say exactly where it had appeared.

The floater would home in on a signal from Tania's suit, the same signal that would be the focus for the returning LMT field when their time was up. If Groombridge's atmosphere had something like a Heaviside layer so that the signal could bounce over the horizon, then it would take only a few minutes for the floater to get to them. If not, the vehicle would have to lift into orbit and quarter the planet, searching for the signal.

A few minutes later, the floater did appear, with an impressive sonic boom. It sensed the positions of all five Tamers and landed a safe distance away—in deep mud, unfortunately.

So Jacque spent his first couple of hours on Groombridge helping the others drag the heavy machine out of the muck, then laboriously scraping it clean.

Tania walked around the glittering floater, inspecting it. "I don't know. The nozzles look clear." It was powered by superheated steam from a fusion mirror; one main jet and eight steering ports. "But I don't have any idea how critical it is. Maybe they could be packed full of mud and still work. Just blast clear."

"Or a small obstruction could start an eddy in the exhaust plasma," Ch'ing said. "Shaking the floater to pieces in one instant."

"Does anybody know for sure?"

Nobody did. "One thing sure," Jacque said. "I want to be someplace else when we start it up. If it goes it'll make a hole big enough to—"

"Oh, the mirror will not blow up," Ch'ing said. "It might break up, but not explode. It has safeguards."

"Okay, you stay here and watch the goddam thing. I'm going to—"

"Look, it's not worth arguing about—"

"*Who's arguing?*"

"Turn down the volume, Jacque!"

Tania continued. "We have to make a preliminary ground survey, anyhow. When we get a few kilometers away, I'll call the floater. If it explodes, we give Jacque a medal. If it homes in, we give Ch'ing a medal."

For the ground survey, the five of them functioned simply as specimen collectors. There was a little box on the front of the GPEM suits that automatically evaluated a specimen as to appearance, density, tensile strength, crystal structure if any, melting and boiling points, chemical composition, presence of microorganisms, and so forth. The data were automatically transmitted to the personnel recorder on Tania's suit.

(The recorder also etched on its data crystals a running record of everybody's body temperature, blood pressure and chemistry, brain waves, respiration, urine and stool analysis, conductivity of skin and mucous membranes, Kirlian field, and hat size. This was not to protect their health—the nearest medical treatment was fourteen light-years away—but to record what had happened in case they were suddenly to die. Which, though the recruiting brochures failed to mention it, was the way most Tamers retired.)

They synchronized their compasses, inertial rather than magnetic, then spread out in a hundred-meter line, east and west, and started plodding north. Anything that looked interesting they picked up and put in the analysis box. Every hundred or so steps they tossed in a handful of dirt or, more often, mud. In this way they formed a fairly complete profile of the geologic and biological properties of a strip of Groombridge one-tenth of a kilometer wide by five long. It wasn't too impressive in the biological department: various kinds of gray plants that were similar enough to known forms not to be exciting, and dissimilar enough from earth plants to cause geoformy headaches.

After about five kilometers, they found a river. The current was sluggish and the water held a fine suspension of light-colored mud. It looked like dirty milk. Along the bank was a jumble of sticky gossamer, pinkish, that turned out to be a form of plant life.

The other side of the river was lost in the fog; it must have been well over a hundred meters away. "Good time to call the floater," Tania said. One thing you couldn't do in a GPEM suit was swim.

A few seconds later she said, "Should be here any—" and the noise of the explosion and the shock wave hit them at the same time. Jacque saw the milky water flying by under his feet—the stabilizer working overtime, buzzing loudly, to keep him upright —and then he touched the surface and skied backwards for a short distance before the water closed over him.

"See, Ch'ing?" he shouted. "What the *fuck* did I tell you?"

"What?" Ch'ing said. He had forgotten their difference of opinion about the floater. "What you say, please?"

"You, uh, never mind." Jacque realized he'd been brooding, like a stubborn boy. And that sneaking spy tapping his bloodstream, ticking off hormones, recording every second of anger and, now, embarrassment.

"Is everybody underwater?" Tania said. There was a jumble of responses. "Wait. Is anybody not underwater?" Everybody was. "Well, let's take a sample of the water and go back."

"God . . . damned sample box is under the mud," Jacque grumbled.

"Then take a sample of the mud," someone said. Jacque did, tight-lipped, then turned on his headlamp and started working his way due south. He couldn't see anything, but it was better to move through bright opaque soup than blackness.

His head broke out of the water and he waited for the lenses to clear. Ch'ing's voice crackled in his earplugs, excited for once:

"I think I have found an animal."

"An animal? How big?"

"Not very big. Fist-sized. It swam in front of me and I caught it." He laughed. "I thought it was a plant, but it wiggles."

Some plants wiggle, Jacque thought. Thanotropism.

Ch'ing surfaced a few meters away, the creature gently cradled in both hands. It looked like a sea urchin, or some such creature, black and spiny. Rippling.

The two of them were on the bank before any of the others came out. "Can I see it, Ch'ing?"

"Of course. Just be careful."

"I'll be careful." Ch'ing handed it to him and there was perhaps one-twentieth of a second when the sensors in both of their suits' "hands" were simultaneously in contact with the animal. During that instant, they heard:

Ch'ing	Jacque
"—goddam Chinaman thinks I'll break his toy, serve him right, if I crush, like in diving, crush and feed to the—"	"—everywhere life even here floating in filth in sterile filth like crush? and feed, is life, yes."

"What?" He almost did drop it.

"Did you say something, please?"

"Hmn." He turned the animal over in his hands. In visible light it was shiny purple, and what had looked like spines were neither stiff nor sharp. They waved with an eery grace that did not suggest panic. "Cilia," Jacque said. "Some kind of cilia. It probably swims with them."

"Perhaps," Ching said. "It does not seem very practical, for locomotion."

"Maybe it's not actually a water animal. It doesn't seem to mind being out of the water."

"You may be right." He took the creature back and when they touched they heard:

CH'ING	JACQUE
"—but it could be dying now	"—but maybe it dies
wiggling like this, like the	this way, graceful
caterpillar in the fire,	slow poem of death like
Mum said, Jacque, you get—	caterpillar? wiggle in
are you reading my mind,	fire? Bad picture,
you are my God reading	splitting, yes, I see
my mind—"	your thoughts and—"

They stared at each other.

11
Bridge I

The Groombridge "bridge": A
Preliminary Statistical Analysis

30 Aug 51

One remarkable property of the ESP-inducing creature Tania Jeeves's team brought back from Groombridge 1618 is that the creature "tunes" itself to individuals. It seems to be most sensitive, or most efficient, with the first person who comes into contact with it, and less sensitive with each subsequent contact.

Further, the sensitivity does not seem to decrease with time.

The effect seems to be the same whether the subject contacts the animal on Groombridge itself, or on Earth. The effect seems to pass through the tactile sensors of the General Purpose Exploration Module without attenuation.

Statistical analysis was done with a standard Rhine test: a deck of fifty cards, ten each of five easily visualized symbols. Each subject "read" the deck ten times through, on three different occasions. The statistical expectation of correct answers, out of 500 trials, would be 100. As the following table shows, the results were compelling:

Subject	partner	26 August Trial	partner	27 August Trial	partner	28 August Trial	Control
1. Lefavre	2	397	3	412	7	388	98
2. Wachal	1	295	3	302	8	270	113
3. Jeeves	1	243	2	257	7	219	104
4. Herrick	1	207	3	228	8	195	133
5. Simone	1	182	2	189	7	170	90
6. Chandler	1	161	3	167	8	156	105
7. Tobias	1	143	2	135	8	140	76
8. Fong	1	131	3	135	7	119	115

The control figure is the individual's score without the Groombridge "bridge," administered by Dr. Chandler or Dr. Fong.

Unfortunately the Tamer who first contacted the bridge (Tamer 1 Hsi Ch'ing) did not survive the mission. The surviving subjects are of the opinion that Ch'ing would have consistently scored 500, as he could literally read their thoughts, word for word.

There seems to be little or no relation between Rhine scores and the identity of the passive partner, the "reader." Lefavre says that he occasionally notices a feedback condition with Wachal: in reading her mind he often "hears" his own thoughts, as interpreted by Wachal. This effect was even stronger with Ch'ing, but Lefavre hasn't noticed it with any of the other Tamers.

Further testing, some of it in a more subjective vein, is being done, mostly on subjects Lefavre and Wachal.

This committee recommends most strongly that another mission be translated to Groombridge 1618, as soon as possible and for as long as possible.

(signed)

Lewis Chandler, Ph.D.
For the Mathematics Committee
General Research Group
AED Colorado Springs

12
Chapter Four

Carol Wachal came out of the muddy water to an unusual sight: Jacque and Ch'ing holding hands.

"What about this animal, Ch'ing . . ." Neither man said anything as she approached them. Then Ch'ing took her hand and gave her the animal, holding on:

CH'ING	CAROL
"—what's the big mystery, why don't they? Funny little thing, what is . . . Ch'ing? Is that you? Are we really talking to each other like this?"	"Mind to mind yes . . . hear thoughts. Hear thoughts. Yes."

"Telepathy," Jacque said. "Pure and simple. Let's try it three ways." He reached out and also touched the creature. Nothing.

Ch'ing withdrew:

JACQUE	CAROL
"—guess it won't work three, you hear me Jacque you hear me Carol? yes I Yes."	"—works again now. You hear me Carol? Yes."

Tania and Vivian splashed ashore some twenty meters downstream. "What are you three babbling about?" Tania said.

They explained rapidly and then demonstrated the creature's powers, first to Tania and then to Vivian.

"Wait," Vivian said. "You say you can talk to each other with this thing?"

"That's right," Ch'ing said. "Complete sentences," Jacque added.

"I don't get anything like that. Ch'ing, you think of something, try it on me and then on Jacque." Ch'ing did.

"All I get," Vivian said, "is 'mountain' and 'rose' . . . and a feeling of sadness, nostalgia."

"Let me try it again," Jacque said. "It's two lines from a poem: 'I haven't seen the Eastern Hill for a long time/How many times has the rose flowered?'"

"That seems to be accurate," Ch'ing said. "It is a poem, a well-known poem by Li Po:

> *Pu chien Tung Shan chiu*
> *Ch'iang-wei chi tu hua.*

The first two lines of the poem, that is."

"You thought it in Chinese?" Jacque said.

"Yes," Ch'ing said.

The five of them stood on the river bank for most of an hour, experimenting. They rejected the first notion, Jacque's, that the creature simply worked better with men than with women. Trying to communicate "hard" data such as Social Security numbers and birth dates, they soon deduced the simple truth: sensitivity of telepathic reception decreased according to how many people had touched the creature before you.

Thus Ch'ing was most sensitive, followed by Jacque, then Carol, Tania, and Vivian, in that order. Ch'ing could read any of them like a book (though actual words came to him in Chinese unless there were no precise equivalent to the English); Vivian received only vague impressions and occasional words. She could get about half the digits in a Social Security number.

"Obviously," Tania said, "it's worth departing from our schedule for a day or two to look for more of these creatures." She suggested they form a line out from the bank, facing the current underwater, with their lights on. They would be able to see the creatures swimming by if they passed within a meter or two.

Ch'ing stayed out of the water to guard "his" creature, while the other four splashed in to find their own.

They talked excitedly for a while, then settled into staring at the bright ochre blankness. Time passed very slowly. It was an event of great interest when a bubble or fragment of twig drifted within Jacque's field of view. He was content, though; there were a lot of things to sort out. He tried to recall each separate link he had made during the course of the past hour's experimentation.

A soft chime told him it was time to eat. He wasn't especially hungry, but was glad to have something to do. The food tube snaked up in front of him and he sucked on it: texture and flavor of mashed potatoes and gravy, but too bland. Then something like an inoffensive mixture of carrots and peas. He wished for a saltshaker. At least the fluids tube gave him a measured amount of red wine.

Now if there were only some way to smuggle in an after-dinner cigar.

Jacque overheard Carol ask Ch'ing whether he would like to try, in the interests of science, an experiment in intimate biological communication, once they got back to Earth with the creature (that being yet another thing you couldn't do inside a GPEM suit). He said he would be delighted and honored.

Jacque did recognize that the wave of jealousy he felt was both unfair and irrational.

After two hours of immersion, which seemed much longer, Tania said they might as well give it up; continue with the survey. Perhaps their presence had frightened the creatures away or, as Vivian suggested, the one that Ch'ing caught had sent out a telepathic warning to the others.

They asked Ch'ing his opinion and got no answer.

While they were scrambling out of the water, Tania called for a readout from Ch'ing's biometrics system. Everything seemed normal except for brain waves: a slight wiggle in theta; no activity at any other level.

Before they reached him, an alarm went off and the following information was projected on her viewplate:

```
EMERGENCY
ALL VITAL FUNCTIONS HAVE CEASED IN GPEM 2
EMERGENCY MEASURES IN EFFECT
UNDIAGNOSED GPEM MALFUNCTION
   NO RESPONSE 21:33:00
   NO RESPONSE 21:33:05
   NO RESPONSE 21:33:10
   NO RESPONSE 21:33:15
   NO RESPONSE 21:33:20
   NO RESPONSE 21:33:25
   NO RESPONSE 21:33:30
DEATH DUE TO CARDIAC ARREST
DEATH PRECEDED BY ABRUPT CESSATION OF MEN-
   TAL ACTIVITY
DEATH DUE TO UNDIAGNOSED GPEM MALFUNCTION
```

13
Insurance Manual

(From *Salesman's Quick Reference to Occupations*, Hartford Insurance Company, Inc., Hartford, CT, 2060:)

Occupation	Recommendations
Tamer	No new policies to be issued.
	Outstanding policies, contracted for previous to current employment, not to be extended.
	Spouse of Tamer also poor risk due to extreme nervous tension. Death to be investigated carefully for possibility of suicide.
	(Actual mortality rates for Tamers are classified information. Informal studies indicate that fewer than 50% survive a tour of duty.)

14
The Slingshot Effect

(Excerpt from an interview with Dr. Jaime Barnett, Research Director, Agency for Extraterrestrial Development, Colorado Springs, at the dedication of the new 120-cm. LMT crystal, 28 October 2044.)

NBC: —now this is something I've never understood. They all come back at the same instant, with no expenditure of power . . .

JB: (laughs) Welcome to the club. Nobody understands it. It's obvious that what's at work here is some kind of a, what scientists call, a conservation law—

NBC: I understand.

JB: —but it's not clear exactly *what* is being conserved. Matter and energy and space-time are all involved. . . . let me stress this. We can describe the Levant-Meyer Translation, we can describe it mathematically to ten significant figures. But it's all empirical; we can't pretend to understand *why* it works.

The Slingshot Effect is itself a good illustration of this. When a group of people is translated to another planet, one of them carries a homing device—what we call their "black box." When their time is up on the planet, everything sufficiently close to the black box will automatically return to Earth.

NBC: How close is "sufficiently close"?

JB: It duplicates exactly the configuration of the original LMT field. In the case of our new crystal here, that will be a cylinder 120 centimeters in diameter by some five meters high.

At any rate, there isn't any theoretical reason for the wiring in this black box to work. Scientists cobbled it together by trial and error, starting from the wiring that was present in the electron microscope that was involved in Levant's original, uh, accidental experiment.

NBC: But only one person can carry this black box.

JB: Of course. The Los Alamos disaster proved that.

NBC: And they can bring back anything they want from the planet, so long as it fits inside the cylindrical field.

JB: That's right, uh, Fred. But as you know, the samples they bring back only stay on earth for as long as the people were on the other planet. Then they disappear.

NBC: They also slingshot back? To their home planet?

JB: That would seem logical. Symmetrical. But we don't know; we've never traced a sample.

NBC: And what happens to a person, on the other planet, if he's caught outside the cylindrical field when time runs out?

JB: That's happened twice. We sent rescue missions both times, but no one was there.

NBC: They just disappeared? It couldn't—

JB: That's right.

NBC: You have no idea what happened to them?

JB: None whatsoever.

Chapter Five

They left Ch'ing's body by the riverside and continued to survey the planet.

Without the floater, it was a difficult task. Most of their time was taken up in traveling—literally running from their high-latitude position up to the pole, down to the equator, and back. With their suits' amplification they could cover a thousand kilometers or more per day.

The planet was less than promising:

There was a sea, covering a fourth of its surface, that had such a high concentration of salt that nothing could live in it, except for certain hardy microorganisms that stayed close to the mouths of rivers.

The polar cap was a frozen wasteland, arid and lifeless, where fossil snow rolled rattling, hard tiny granules pushed by a never-ceasing gale; where the wind carved ice mountains into fantastic shapes, great curving sweeps that met in razor edges to sing one long note in the wind.

A chain of dead volcanos, their tops dusted with a golden snow of monoclinic sulphur.

An ancient weathered meteor crater, larger than Texas, perfectly round, with the vestige of a central peak—filled with sweet water and a bewildering variety of marine life. None of the creatures had telepathic properties.

Working down from the pole, the frozen sterile ground thawed into a bog, with more and more plant life as they moved toward the equator; then less life as the ground dried out and the temperature rose. The last several hundred kilometers before the equator was all parched desolation, bare gray rock and sand in monotonously regular dunes.

On their last day they hurried back to the river, so they

could slingshot Ch'ing's corpse and suit back for the scientists at Colorado Springs.

DEATH DUE TO UNDIAGNOSED GPEM MALFUNC-TION had haunted all of them for seven days. They had been pushing their suits to the limit all week. Ch'ing had been killed by his just standing, doing nothing.

But there hadn't been any problems. These things happen, Tania said; freak accidents. The GPEM's are checked, double-, triple-, and quadruple-checked. But it's as complex a mechanism as anyone has ever trusted with his life. The doctors and engineers will find out what happened to Ch'ing and make sure it never happens again. Tania said.

The river had risen and Ch'ing was standing upright in knee-deep water. They got there with more than two hours to spare, before the Slingshot Effect took hold.

They moved him out of the water and sat, waiting. Jacque took the creature out of the compartment in Ch'ing's suit, where they had stored it (in an environment that simulated the river).

They passed the animal around and its powers seemed undiminished.

"I have a theory," Jacque said.

"On what?" Carol said.

"Why there aren't any land animals." Except for the creature Ch'ing found, they'd found no animal that could survive out of the water. "When that meteor hit, you know, the big crater? It must have caused a worldwide catastrophe. Earthquakes, fires, tidal waves—"

"Fill the atmosphere with superheated steam, if it landed in water," Carol said.

"Radioactive steam," Tania added. "That kind of impact—"

"That's what I mean," Jacque said. "Nothing on land survived. Only plants and animals that were protected by a buffer of water."

"Could be, could well be," Tania said. "If that happened, the geologists ought to be able to reconstruct it."

"From the samples," Carol said.

They were quiet for some time. The only one standing was Ch'ing.

"How much longer?" Vivian asked.

"About twenty minutes," Tania said. "Twenty-two."

Another long silence. "Well, we might as well get into position," Tania said. "Jacque, you'll be on top again, otherwise the heights won't match up. I'll be on the bottom with Ch'ing . . . Ch'ing's suit."

They shuffled and climbed into place, after Tania scratched a 120-centimer circle to guide their arms and legs. "Four minutes."

Like the first time, the transition was abrupt. One instant, they were looking out over the dirty-milk river; the next instant they were falling from a meter or so above the floor of the Colorado Springs LMT chamber.

"We have life," Vivian said, before Jacque had even hit the ground. "Need a chamber at twenty-eight degrees, pressure point eight nine four. The following mix: nitrogen, point three fiive seven; argon, point two nine seven . . ." This would be the preliminary environment for the creature; they would be able to match the ambience of Groombridge exactly after analyzing the samples the Tamers brought back. ". . . and a source of circulating water, a tub. The creature is semiaquatic."

"And we have a fatality, Tamer Ch'ing. Undiagnosed suit malfunction."

Before going through decontamination, they had to wait for an analysis team to come take charge of their samples. It took a while, since most of the scientists had to be routed out of bed—nobody had expected a milk-run training mission to come back with organic material.

The autopsy team, though, was ready and waiting.

Finally they went through the room of mirrors and cleansing lights, into the ready room. The cranes lifted off the top halves of their GPEM's and they scrambled out to an orgy of backscratching. Then hot showers and clean clothes, a quick physical exam and some real food. Then six hours of rest before debriefing, while the analysts surveyed their accumulated data.

Jacque set down the totally naked bone of a ravaged pork chop. "Uh, Carol . . ."

"Sure. Should be fun." She poured herself another glass of wine and passed the carafe down to Vivian.

"You know—"

"I've been waiting an hour for you to ask."

"And I've been waiting for you. After all, you asked Ch'ing."

"He would never have gotten around to it. I was curious how long it would take you."

Jacque raised his glass. "In the interests of science, then."

She joined him. "Pure research."

"One of you lovebirds pass the salt?"

16
Autopsy

TO: Medical Research Group, AED Colorado Springs, West-
     hampton, Lyon, Nagpur, Mengtzu, La Rioja, Charleville

FROM: Johnathon Legman, M.D., Ph.D.
      Andre Barnett, M.D.
      Miriam Kophage, M.D., Medical Research Group,
      AED Col Spr

RE: Autopsy of Tamer 1 Hsi Ch'ing

Abstract
Tamer 1 Hsi Ch'ing died on his first translation, a training
mission to a fairly earthlike planet of Groombridge 1618. The
mission was highly unusual in many respects. Not only was the
planet quite viable for geoformy, but one of the animals the
Tamers discovered seems to function as an amplifier for telepathic communication (preliminary report attached; Appendix
VIII).

Tamer Ch'ing died at 21:32:47.6, 17 August 2051. The
GPEM attempted to diagnose the cause of death but was unable
to, and so communicated to the supervisor "Death due to undiagnosed GPEM malfunction," and then froze the cadaver for
later analysis earthside.

Our bioengineering section has checked out the GPEM very
minutely, and reports that it is functioning perfectly. Its data
crystals show no indication of malfunction at the time of the
Tamer's death. The diagnostic it communicated to the supervisor
can also be interpreted "Cause of death unknown." (Appendix
III)

Our examination of the cadaver was similarly negative.
Tamer Ch'ing was in excellent health on 20 August 2051 (See

pre-translation physical, Appendix IV), and the cadaver likewise showed no symptoms of illness or trauma not directly at-
tributable to postmortem freezing.

Biometric data just prior to death are ambiguous, and can
be variously interpreted as indicating death due to cardiac in-
farction or massive cerebrovascular incident. Autopsy, however,
denies the possibility of either.

28 August 2051

Contents:
Autopsy report

Copies of original data crystals available on request.

17
Schedule

EXPERIMENT SCHEDULE: Groombridge "Bridge."

	Hours	Team	Purpose	Equipment
	25 Aug 03:05		(translation)	—
	03:05—10:00	Senior Survey	General investigation	ad lib
	10:00—17:00	Bio Group, Willard	Meta/catabolic meas.	Mod. Stokes chamber
	17:00—24:00	Bio Group, Jameson	Reaction to stimuli	ad lib
26 Aug	00:00—14:00	Math Comm, Chandler	ESP (stat)	Rhine deck
	14:00—15:00	PR Group	Public relations	ad lib
	15:00—22:00	Bio Group, Van der Walls	Exp. w/terrestrial animals	modified breathers, animals ad lib.
	22:00—24:00	Lefavre, Wachal	Personal (ESP, psych)	cot
27 Aug	00:00—14:00	Math Comm, Fong	ESP (stat)	Rhine deck
	14:00—17:00	Riley et al	Press Conference	—
	17:00—24:00	Bio Group, Willard	Change in metabolic rate wrt stress incre- ment	Mod. Stokes chamber

EXPERIMENTS 28 AUG–31 AUG TO BE DETERMINED BY
RESULTS OF THE PRECEDING WORK.

1 Sept	19:00—20:49	Bio Group, Willard	Dissection	Surg instr., cameras
	20:49	—	(translation: "sling- shot")	

18
Chapter Six: Prelude

> *A preliminary to an action, event,*
> *condition, or work of broader scope and*
> *higher importance . . . an independent*
> *piece of moderate length, sometimes used*
> *as an introduction to a fugue . . .*

SETTING: The finest restaurant in Colorado Springs, Saturday evening, 26 August 2051. JACQUE LEFAVRE has invited CAROL WACHAL to dinner. Candlelight, heavy velvet, music by a neoElizabethan octet. The waiter has taken the dishes away; JACQUE orders from the wine steward a bottle of Château d' Yquem 2039.

Teasing:

> CAROL
> Am I really worth that much?

A little defensive:

> JACQUE
> It's an occasion.

> CAROL
> Won't be much of an occasion if we drink too much. Alcohol *is* a depressant.

> JACQUE
> Good wine never hurt that . . . facility.

> CAROL
> Are you always so formal?

> JACQUE
> Me? I'm not so—

> CAROL
> Yes you are. You've been treating me like a cousin you haven't seen in a long time. Not like—

> JACQUE
> Well, hell. Maybe I'm a little nervous. It's not your usual first date.
>
> CAROL
> That's true. Loosen up, though. It's not as if we'll be on a stage in front of—
>
> JACQUE
> Yeah.
>
> I'm glad you stepped in when old Chandler wanted us to—

Shrugs.

> CAROL
> There are limits.
>
> JACQUE
> I suspect you weren't quite as outraged as you acted, though.
>
> CAROL
> Don't pry, now. You'll have your chance later.

Laughs.

> JACQUE
> I suppose. Here comes our man.

The wine steward serves the bottle with appropriate ceremony. They toast and drink.

> CAROL
> Good.
>
> Are you used to this kind of living?
>
> JACQUE
> Was once. Not since I was a boy.
>
> CAROL
> Your parents were rich?
>
> JACQUE
> Fairly well off. Dad was a senior physicist at Institut Fermi in New York.

CAROL
He's dead now.

Hesitates.

JACQUE
In a manner of speaking. Let's talk about something else.

CAROL
Sure, I'm sorry.

JACQUE
It's funny.

CAROL
Hmm?

JACQUE
Well . . . that we should have gone through so much together—discover a new world together—and be such strangers.

CAROL
Together separately. I can't get used to seeing you as a solid human, inside a body. You're supposed to be just a voice in my ear.

JACQUE
I don't have any trouble getting used to your body.

CAROL
You're so gallant.

JACQUE dips a forefinger in the wine and skims along the top of the glass. It's fine crystal and makes a pure singing note, which unfortunately doesn't go well with the octet. A man at the next table gives JACQUE a sharp look, and he stops.

CAROL
You don't care for the music?

JACQUE
Music! It's just a gimmick to sell lutes and flutes.

CAROL
It's pretty . . .

JACQUE
Next year it'll be electric guitars.

CAROL
Could be.

JACQUE
If it were real Elizabethan music, madrigals and such, that would be all right—austere, controlled; but this modern—

CAROL
Calm down, Jacque. It's nothing to get all worked up over.

JACQUE finishes his wine and pours another glass. CAROL declines.

CAROL
What time is it?

JACQUE
Five after nine . . .

CAROL
If we left now, we could walk to the chamber.

JACQUE
That's . . .

Regards his drink.

probably a good idea.

Signals waiter.

It's a nice night.

JACQUE settles the check and they leave, CAROL's hand lightly on his arm.

19
Fugue

*A polyphonic composition based
upon one, two, or more themes, which
are enunciated by several voices or
parts in turn, subjected to a contrapuntal
treatment, and gradually built
up into a complex form having somewhat
distinct divisions or stages of development
and a marked climax at the end.*

The Groombridge bridge was housed in a room-sized hyperbaric chamber adjacent to the ready room. It was overbuilt for the purpose, the air pressure on Groombridge being nine-tenths of an atmosphere, but as Jacque pointed out, it had one real advantage for their particular experiment: no windows.

They were a little early, and were sharing a cup of coffee when Van der Walls and his group came out.

"Any results, Dr. Van?" Carol asked.

"Difficult to say." He shook his head. "Most of the animals were lethargic." He opened the cage he was carrying and took out a small collie, still trailing wires from its head and chest. It was limp as a rag; didn't want to stand. Van der Walls stroked it gently and talked to it.

"They couldn't wear masks, of course. Carbon dioxide got to most of them. We'll know more after we look at the biometrics results. There, boy." The dog was standing sleepily.

His two assistants brought out the rest of the cages. "That's it, Van," one of them said. Van der Walls tucked the dog under his arm and with a straight face wished them good luck.

Jacque and Carol put new plastic inserts in two of the breathers and slipped on the masks. They didn't strap the tanks on their backs, but carried them through the airlock into the chamber.

The drop in pressure made their ears pop.

"Not exactly the honeymoon suite," Jacque said. Bright white enamel walls and black tile floor, an aquarium full of muddy water on a table in the middle. A folding cot borrowed from the infirmary. Video cameras.

"*Omnia vincit Amor*," Carol said.

"We'll see." They led each other to the cot. In passing, Jacque threw his jacket over one of the cameras.

"They said the cameras wouldn't be on," Carol said.

Jacque was taking his shirt off, a tricky business, since it was a turtleneck. He had to worry it over the mask, then thread it down over the airhose and tank. "That's what they said." He threw the shirt over the other camera.

Carol's semiformal jumpsuit presented no problem. She ran her finger down the seam and shrugged it off, folded it neatly and set it on the table by the aquarium. She smiled at him, groped through the murky water and fished out the bridge. It was wet, but not slimy.

"This should be fun." She sat down next to him on the cot. He stroked her gently, made no move to touch the bridge.

She stretched out on the cot, put her head in his lap, lifted her mask enough to kiss him, then lick.

He ruffled her short hair. "You don't waste time."

"I don't feel like wasting time." She urged him down. While they were shifting, making room on the narrow cot, they touched the bridge:

JACQUE	CAROL
Disconcertingly	"But quick so
accurate closeup	quick . . ." *Blurred*
of his face, then	*picture of various*
genitals super-	*parts of her body,*

JACQUE	CAROL
imposed "So nervous he is, so solid."	*shifting* "Skin hot."

"I'm not nervous," he said in a hoarse whisper.

"Of course not." She ran a finger down his chest. "Hair's growing back."

"Have to—hey!"

"Sorry, ticklish?"

"Only the navel, never could . . . that's better."

"I should hope." She put his hand on her breast and touched the bridge again.

JACQUE	CAROL
Her eyes closed he sees dark red feels fingers bump over hard nipple pleasure two places "Think something sexy" . . .NOT THINK See her mind see his hand "What not think?"	*Her face the sudden curve of her hip* "So hot, soft, so like . . . so like . . . not to think, not to think . . ." *His hand moving over her breast* A BEACH IN BRIGHT SUN A SLENDER GIRL "Not to think Maria not to think . . ."

"Don't censor yourself," she said softly. "She looks like me? In your mind she does."

"Did." He traced a line with his finger, down her ribs, waist, hard bump of her hipbone.

JACQUE	CAROL
Warm wake of pleasure follows	*Sliding down hot damp skin* "See her jump" *and*

JACQUE	CAROL
his finger belly	*over sandpapery stubble*
jumps in nervous	*down alongside it stop then*
reflex "O hurry O	*part lips from bottom so*
hurry" over the	*hot so wet slide up and*
little tendon	*find it* MARIA RUNNING
corner and down—	UP FROM THE WATER SHE
"There O now	SITS ON MY BLANKET
hurry" lips part-	DRYING HAIR LEGS APART
ing wet sound	PINK MYSTERY IN BLONDE HALO
breath holding	"No bad boy" slippery
"There O no too	*here* "Too hard? I . . ."
hard O—here	
BAD BOY here!"	

"Here." She let go of the bridge for a second to position his hand.

JACQUE	CAROL
"Still now." *she*	"So ready!"
thrusts against	"Don't press
him twice breath-	she knows still now."
ing once deep	
anus tightening	"I . . ."
"O . . Oh" *away*	"How can . . ."
and back again	
slow featherlight	"?"
circling touch	
" . . ."	"Jesus!"
hot pulses two	
" . . ."	
three diminishing	
" . . . Oh."	
radiate tingling	
" . . . Oh, Jacque."	

"Oh, Jacque." She rubbed her forehead against his chest, wiping off sweat. He let go of the bridge to hold her tightly.

He swallowed twice. "You don't need much warming up, do you?"

She giggled into his chest. "It's been over a week. Can't touch yourself in a suit."

"You had all day," he said.

"Saved it." She resumed rubbing him. "Is this all right?"

"Fine." He glided the edge of his hand down her backbone, skin slick and cooling. "That was . . . something." His fingers rested lightly at the top of the crevice between her buttocks, his thumb making little circles in a lumbar dimple. "It's different than with men."

"Better?"

"Different."

She stopped panting. "It wouldn't be so fast . . . but the bridge! It's like . . . it's like . . . being both people. Not quite that, something like that. Exciting."

It wasn't like that for Jacque. "Good, good." For Jacque, it was like being watched.

"We don't have to hold on to the bridge with our hands," she said. "How about this?" She rolled over so her back was toward Jacque. "Take me longer this way." She reached over her shoulder and slipped the bridge between her back and Jacque's chest.

JACQUE	CAROL
"If I try think about something else" *feel of him wilting on her* "CRAWLY TRAPPED SPIDER"	*soft nest* "God! crawly bug trapped spider get it away!"

He almost pushed her off the cot, squirming away from contact with the bridge. "I'm sorry, it . . . let's just hold on to it with our hands. Then we can drop it if—"

"You felt trapped."

"*It* was trapped."

She reached back to hold him. "Jacque, you aren't afraid of me, are you? Afraid to let me inside—"

"No. No, I like it." Not a complete lie. "Just let's keep the bridge . . . at arm's length. I don't like it touching me. I don't like it so close."

"All right." She set the creature by her abdomen. "Can you reach it here?"

"Yeah." They touched the bridge and with her free hand she guided him into her.

JACQUE	CAROL
"There" *pushing*	*Quick shiver good*
back him warm	*going in then slight*
against her "Tell	*resistance overcome*
now Maria"	*buttocks surprising cold*
NO CAN'T *staying*	"No I can't" *staying*
then slow then	*then drawing back slowly*
fast, holding	*and quick thrust hold-*
tense	*ing tense* "All right"

"All right." Both of them eyes closed, faces flushed. Carol stroking him gently, "I trust you," he said:

JACQUE	CAROL
Hot wet Trust	"Trust you" SITTING ON
"She is like me	MY BLANKET DRYING HAIR
with hair—"	LEGS APART SHE LOOKING
slick cold outside	AWAY THEN LOOK DOWN AND
going in slow hard	SEE ME HARD THEN WHAT
HARD *out quick*	REALLY HAPPEN SHE LAUGH AND
in slow	SAY YOU GROWING UP JACQUES
out	AND PAT MY KNEE AND RUN
in	AWAY DOWN THE SAND
"But Jacque	LAUGHING BUT I ALWAYS

JACQUE	CAROL
you not here"	REMEMBER THERE'S NOBODY
in, out in, "Feel	ELSE THERE AND WE PLAY
ME Jacque," *out in*	TOGETHER AND SHE ON TOP OF
SHE ON TOP	ME ON THE BLANKET
I LOVED SHE	SHE SHOWS ME
DIED	HOW
"Jacque"	"I loved her she was my
	sister she died"

"She died when . . . I was twelve when she died."

"Jacque." She reached blindly back and touched his cheek, eyes. "My poor Jacque."

They tried five different sexual geometries in the next hour, Carol becoming fairly exhausted after nine or ten orgasms. Jacque was even more exhausted by the strain of none.

He could start but he couldn't finish. Not with another person's thoughts, however attractive, intruding on his privacy; not with his own fantasies being reflected back to him distorted by Carol's sympathies—and by her revulsion sometimes, though she tried to mask it.

Carol had no such problems: she was not a very private person to begin with, and she was less sensitive to the bridge. Being tuned in to Jacque was a delicious spice to her, like making love surrounded by mirrors, with an illustrated pornographic story unreeling in her mind.

Carol lay panting on the couch. Jacque picked up the bridge, walked stiffly over to the aquarium, and dropped the creature into its water. He retrieved his jacket from the camera and sat down next to Carol.

"We forgot towels," he said, and began patting her dry.

She made a purring sound and stretched. "You don't want to—"

"No. I've had it."

"There's plenty of time." The clock said 23:14. "If we did it without the bridge you—"

"Please."

"I was just—"

"Carol, some other time I'd love to but *some other time!*"

She flinched. "Don't be mad at me."

"I'm not mad at you."

"Don't be mad at yourself either. You couldn't help—"

"Let's not talk. Let's just not talk."

"All right." She tried to dry him but he twisted away and went to get dressed. She turned her back to him and rummaged through her purse for a tissue.

20
Coda

A more or less independent passage,
at the end of a composition,
introduced to bring it to a satisfactory close.

They had eight hours before they were due back at the chamber for Rhine testing. Jacque walked with Carol back to her cottage. It was a misty summer's-end night, clouds rolling in heavy with rain, heat lightning on the horizon. They walked apart and didn't say much.

She took his hand and held on while she thumbed the door open. "I don't have anything to drink in the—"

"Carol, uh, look. I'm sorry. It wasn't you. It was that damned—"

"Shush." She slipped her arms around him and leaned her head on his chest. After a moment: "I owe you a meal, Lefavre."

"Oh, that—"

"Free for breakfast tomorrow?" Tugging him toward the door. "Come on. I have real eggs."

21
To the Marriage of True Minds Admit Impediments

The Effect of Telepathic
Communion on Coitus
by
Raymond Sweeney, M.D., Ph.D.

HIGHLY CONFIDENTIAL

1. It is not meant to be implied that any general conclusions may be drawn from this report, based as it is on one single episode. Certain aspects of it, however, may be of interest to investigators of human sexual function and dysfunction.

2. The subjects involved were Jacque (sic) L. and Carol W., the two veterans of the first Groombridge mission most sensitive to the amplifying effect of the Groombridge bridge. They were scheduled for two hours' sexual experimentation in conjunction with the bridge, without observation, on the condition that they consent to interviews afterward.

3. The subjects seem sexually compatible, but had no mutual sexual relationship prior to the experiment (in retrospect, this seems unfortunate). Neither has any significant history of dysfunction. Carol's testimony reveals a relatively high frequency of sexual contacts; Jacque's, relatively low.

4. The subjects were interviewed separately for two to three hours, two days after the experiment. Carol allowed part of the interview to be conducted under hypnosis; Jacque did not.

5. Carol reported a relatively normal, if unusually intense

and accelerated, pattern of sexual response. Jacque suffered acute ejaculatory incompetence.

6. Jacque recalled two previous episodes of ejaculatory incompetence, both with well-defined etiology: unusual fatigue, overindulgence in alcohol, lack of emotional rapport with his partner (a prostitute, when he was sixteen). He claims that none of these factors was present to any significant degree in this case, and attributes the episode entirely to the influence of the bridge.

7. Carol, on the other hand, would like to have a bridge of her own.

8. Directly following the experiment, the couple twice shared mutually enjoyable coitus, which of course reinforces Jacque's claim.

9. Transcripts of the interviews, and medical histories, are here appended.

22
Sing Nonnie

(From *A Critical History of American Popular Music*, Volume 6 [2040–2060], by Eliot Green. Copyright © Quadrangle TFX, 2072.)

. . . briefly dominated by a bastard creation baptised the "NeoElizabetham Movement."

The instruments were Elizabethan—as well as copies could be made with 21st Century craftsmachineship—and the melodies and many of the words were stolen from that period. But the spirit behind it was pure profit, merchants and musicians alike cashing in on the blunted sensibilities of a novelty-hungry public.

A typically bad example is "Sweet Lovers Love the Spring," popular in the fall of that year:

Not a complete stanza, but could anyone care? Musically, it's unimaginative—and the words have an immediate emetic effect on any lover of Shakespeare.

Rumor has it that the song was written by a computer in the Public Relations department of the Agency for Extraterrestrial Development. . . .

23
Chapter Seven

Jacque closed the briefing room door behind him and nodded hello to everyone. He took a seat beside Carol. The soft leather creaking was the only sound in the room.

"Okay," Tania said, looking up from her clipboard. "We're all here. Jacque, this is our new teammate, Gustav Hasenfel, from Bremehauven. Jacque Lefavre."

Jacque leaned over the seminar table to shake hands. "*Guten Tag.*" Pale blond hair, handsome strong features, tall, ineffable sadness in clear blue eyes. Handshake warm, dry, firm. Jacque did not like him.

"*'Tag. Sind Schweizer?*"

"*Ja naturlich. Mein Akzent?*"

"*Jawohl.*"

"Hey," Carol said. "Speak French or something."

"Gus is a Tamer Two," Tania said. "He's had four missions." Which meant, Jacque knew, that after his last mission retirement and/or death had reduced his team to two or three. Otherwise they wouldn't have broken up his team; the AED liked to keep people together.

"Now," Tania said, tapping the clipboard. "Two things; three things. Jacque and Gus, they're tapping you for a breeding mission. Day after tomorrow, September second, 0536."

"My poor overworked boy," Carol whispered, humorlessly.

"Where will it be?" Gus asked.

"Sixty-one Cygni B. Fascinating place."

"Indeed. We spent two months there, geoforming."

She smiled. "I had a baby there last year."

"I missed you by three years, then."

Short silence while they nodded at each other. "The rest of us won't be going out until next month. They did manage to fund another Groombridge expedition, a longer one. We'll be there forty-seven days, starting October eleventh. With the mass spectrograph."

"Starting geoformy?" Vivian asked.

"Probably not. The preliminary analysis is that Groombridge would be more trouble than it's worth. What we're to do, eventually, is set up a few buildings for a psychic research center. This mission is just to look for bridges. And isolate elements for an engineering team that'll follow in a couple of weeks.

"They'll have our work plans printed by the last week in September. Everybody except Jacque and Gus is on leave until the twenty-fifth."

"How long is the breeding mission?" Jacque said.

"Twenty hours. Oh, here." She tossed him a small plastic vial. "Take one every six hours, starting midnight tonight. And be a good boy." She arched one eyebrow.

"Starting midnight," Carol said.

Tania laughed. "Starting midnight. Don't wear him out, though.

"Today the bridge slingshots back. They're going to dissect it, starting nineteen hundred. Anybody who wants to watch is invited."

Carol raised her hand. "Have they found out how Ch'ing died?"

"No. Depends on who you ask. Medical group says it has to have been the suit. Bioengineering says no. They're still working on it."

"That's comforting," Carol said.

Tania shrugged. "It's happened before. I don't know who to believe. Just hoping it wasn't the suit.

"We'll have a meeting on the twenty-fifth. Check your mailbox a few days before that; we'll have some sort of preliminary research summary. The math committee and bio group have already published some findings, if you want to look them up.

"Otherwise, you're free for a month. How many want to come to the dissection?" Everybody except Carol raised his hand; then she raised hers. "Fine, I'll tell them. See you there."

Jacque and Carol walked into town for an early supper. The Mexican restaurant wasn't good, but it was better than the AED cafeteria.

"Why don't we just skip the dissection?" Carol said after they'd ordered. "Spend a quiet evening at home."

He laughed. "You act like I'm going off on some long journey."

"Well, you are."

"For less than a day." He stirred the ice in his water glass. "Actually, I think you're jealous."

"I am *not*. Don't be silly."

"I don't mean jealous of this particular woman. I mean the situation. That you have to stay in one place and make babies while I . . . flit around the galaxy like a horny butterfly."

"I don't brood on it." He smiled at her pun. "Besides, it's safer."

"Do you know how long it'll be before they . . ."

"Breed me? No. Tania says I ought to get at least two more regular jumps first. Then, if I follow her pattern, they'll keep me pregnant for several years."

"She had six?"

"Yes. But that's unusual." The waiter brought their plates: refried beans and some meatlike substance.

"If I were a girl I wouldn't be too enthusiastic about it."

"You get to meet lots of interesting men." She tasted the food and then spooned hot sauce all over it. "What do you think of Gus?"

"He's all right, I guess."

She laughed. "The hell you say. If you could've seen you two sizing each other up . . ."

"Come on. I haven't had two words with him."

"Sure," she said softly. "Did you hear what happened to him?"

"What?"

"We're his third team. The first one, four people disappeared. Went out on a floater, and a little while later the super got four simultaneous death readings. Floater came back without a scratch on it."

"That's creepy enough. Find out what happened?"

"Never. No bodies, no suits, nothing. That was Seventy Ophiuchi A, about two years ago. The other was a geoformy accident, last year, Tau Ceti. Some kind of explosion killed half his team."

"How do you know all this?"

"I get to briefing sessions early."

They ate in silence for a while. Jacque poured the last of his beer. "Poor Gus," he said. "Good thing we're not superstitious."

"Isn't it, though."

It was standing room only in the hyperbaric chamber, some thirty people keeping out of the way of Willard's Bio Group and the holo team that was setting up to record the dissection.

A reporter from Science-News TFX asked Dr. Willard whether they would be looking for some particular feature.

"Actually, we don't know exactly what we're looking for. What it'll look like, that is. Obviously what we want is the organ responsible for its special talent.

"We've done neutron and neutrino scans on the creature; X-ray movies, you name it. As far as we can tell, it has no more nervous system than a grape. It's little more than a hollow tube that takes food in at one end and expels waste at the other. And lets people read minds."

He opened a black case and began to lay out glittering tools on the table in front of him. "There won't be any anaesthetic. If you'll check your data summary, that's experiment eleven, twenty-six August. As far as we could tell, nothing causes the creature pain. I don't have any explanation for this. Even protozoa respond to trauma.

"Are Jacque Lefavre and Carol Wachal here?"

They raised their hands. "Come on up, please. . . . Would you mind helping out a little here?"

"Not at all," Jacque said. Carol nodded. "We're not sterile, though."

"That's all right, neither am I." To the reporter: "Lefavre and Wachal are the two Tamers most sensitive to the bridge effect.

"This is Dr. Jameson's suggestion. We want the two Tamers to stay in contact with the bridge as the experiment proceeds. Hopefully, you'll be able to tell us at what stage of the dissection the creature loses its power. And give us some subjective impression of, oh, the rate at which the power declines, whether it might peak or otherwise fluctuate . . . and so forth. All right?"

"We'll try," Jacque said. Carol was a little pale. As she'd told him on the way back from supper, she had an irrational fear of watching dissections. When she was five or six she'd seen a popular science show where they'd taken the heart out of a living turtle and kept it beating for weeks. She still had nightmares about that heart.

They positioned the two Tamers so they wouldn't get in the way of the holo cameras. When they touched the bridge, Jacque caught the racing fear in Carol's mind. He tried to radiate reassurance, tenderness. He only half-heard what Dr. Williard was saying.

"Nobody's ever dissected one of these before, of course. The nudibranch, though, is a close structural analog." He picked up a scalpel. "Accordingly, I will . . . I . . . will make a sss—will incision, hm. Along the dors-dors'l service . . ."

"Doctor—" An aide reached toward him.

The scalpel clattered on the table. With a puzzled expression on his lined face, Williard clutched his chest and sat down on the floor. He fell over sideways without straightening.

The aide felt for a pulse. "Heart stopped," he said. He ripped open the front of Williard's tunic.

"*Get him out of here!*" Dr. Jameson shouted. "Get him out in the hall, oxygen, *you*—" He pointed at another aide. "—call a floater!"

There was a lot of confusion, shouting, shoving through the crowd. Jameson asked that everybody except medical doctors stay inside the chamber until they got Willard on his way to the hospital.

After a few minutes, Jameson came back inside. He stood in front of the table and addressed the group.

"This is a terrible . . . thing. I've been after Bob—" He pointed at the reporter. "This isn't for publication. I've been after Bob for ten years or more to go get an implant, a cardiac implant. An eighty-year-old man who smokes and drinks the way he does . . . well, most of you know Bob. He said he'd get an implant the day he stopped playing tennis.

"They got here in four minutes and there's a cardiac team scrubbed and waiting back at General. So they might be able to save him.

"Meanwhile . . . I'd like to keep posted on Bob, but we have less than an hour to finish up here, before the thing sling-shots. So on with it."

He went to the other side of the table and picked up the scalpel Willard had dropped. "Now I don't claim to know half the invertebrate anatomy that Bob does. Is there anybody here who thinks they can do a better job?"

Nobody responded. "Speak up, God damn it. I'm not pulling rank here. How about you, Modibo? You did that damn slug last month."

A big black man in the front of the crowd shook his head slowly. "Not out of any special expertise, doctor. I was just on deck at the right time."

"You go ahead, Phil," another said. "If we see anything, we'll shout it out."

"All right." To Carol and Jacque: "You two grab hold of the thing.

"Now. Dorsal incision." He brought the blade down and hesitated. "Hm. *Dorsal*."

He looked up at Jacque and shook his head violently. Then he carefully raised the scalpel and slit his own throat.

24
Geoformy II: Access to Tools

To: Public Relations, Westinghouse International
From: Black & Morgenstern
Date: 11 November 2075
Subject: Text and Preliminary Camera Instructions, Four-Minute Public Interest Spot (for midpoint insert, Don Loft Show, 17 Jan 76)

SETTING: Craters of the Moon National Park
REQUIREMENTS: Animation lab; three (3) available-light holo cameras, three (3) actors, two (2) simulated GPEM suits, one (1) Westinghouse mass spectrograph.

Spot begins with a 30-second animated cartoon. First you have a simplified alien landscape, strange music. Five Tamers °pop° into existence, get out of formation and mill around, waiting.

The place they appeared from goes °pop° again, this time producing a pile of bricks, mortar, bricklaying tools. Music segues into a soft jissto as they start building a house. Tempo increases as they work faster and faster. New piles of bricks appear °pop° as they need them; it takes four piles to finish the house.

The Tamer-figures sit around the house, panting. Suddenly the music stops and the bottom layer of bricks disappears. The top three-fourths of the house falls with a resounding crash. This is repeated three more times, as each successive layer disappears.

The Tamers stand there scratching their heads. Then they also disappear. Fade into Craters of the Moon sequence.

(Camera positions given in conventional Cartesian style. Primary origin is ground level, centered underneath mass spectrograph, which will be placed on a level area 1250 meters NNW of benchmark 1728 (permissions bought from Park Service, Inc.). X-axis oriented 29° E of N. initially.)

time	origin	skew	X	Y	Z
030	31,00,3	00	8.5,8.5,3.0		
035	31,00,3	00	8.5,8.5,3.0		

SLOW X-AXIS DRIFT TO

time	origin	skew	X	Y	Z
045	10,00,2	00	8.5,8.5,3.0		
050	05,05,1	00	8.5,8.5,3.0		
055	00,00,0	00	7.5,7.5,3.0		

TIGHTEN TO

time	origin	skew	X	Y	Z
065	00,00,0	00	2.0,2.0,2.0		

SKEW ROLL

time	origin	skew	X	Y	Z
075	00,00,0	−180	1.5,1.5,2.0		

HOLD THIS
CONFIGURATION TO

time	origin	skew	X	Y	Z
101	00,00,0	−180	1.5,1.5,2.0		

SLOW
SQUEEZE/SKEW/DROP

time	origin	skew	X	Y	Z
102	00,00,0	−175	1.4,1.4,1.9		
103	00,00,0	−170	1.3,1.3,1.9		
104	00,00,0	−166	1.2,1.2,1.8		
105	00,00,0	−163	1.1,1.1,1.8		
106	00,00,0	−161	1.0,1.0,1.7		
107	00,00,0	−159	0.9,0.9,1.7		
108	00,00,0	−158	0.9,0.9,1.6		
109	00,00,0	−157	0.9,0.9,1.6		
110	00,00,0	−156	0.9,0.9,1.6		

Shattered landscape.
VOICE OVER:

(t = 33) "Nothing made on the Earth can stay on another planet."

(t = 55) "This is the machine that gave humankind the stars."

(t = 70) "The Westinghouse . . . Mass Spectrograph."

(t = 72) The two Tamers, walking together, approach the machine. They are carrying great armloads of rock, which they dump onto an already-large pile beside the machine.

VOICE OVER:
(t = 88) "They don't use the Westinghouse Mass Spectrograph to build brick houses. They use it to isolate pure elements . . . to build the machines . . .

time	origin	skew	X Y Z
111	00,00,0	−155	0.9,0.9,1.6
112	00,00,0	−154	0.9,0.9,1.6
113	00,00,0	−153	0.9,0.9,1.6

BLUR SKEW:

| 114 | 00,00,0 | −098 | 0.9,0.9,1.6 |

HOLD THIS
CONFIGURATION TO

| 122 | 00,00,0 | −098 | 0.9,0.9,1.6 |

OUT AND SLIGHT UP
(clear rock pile)

123	00,00,0	−098	1.0,1.0,1.7
124	00,00,0	−098	1.2,1.2,1.8
125	00,00,0	−098	1.4,1.4,1.9
126	00,00,0	−098	1.7,1.7,1.9
127	00,00,0	−098	2.1,2.1,1.9
128	00,00,0	−098	2.7,2.7,2.0
129	00,00,0	−098	3.5,3.5,2.0

HOLD THIS
CONFIGURATION TO

| 143 | 00,00,0 | −098 | 3.5,3.5,2.0 |

SLOW SKEW
(to other side of machine)

144		−096	
145		−094	
146		−092	
147		−090	
148		−088	
149		−086	
150		−084	

that will turn this sterile world . . . into a paradise for future generations."

(t = 114) "This bank of dials and switches is a thing that ancient alchemists sought for all their lives: the Philosopher's Stone.

(BEAT to t = 125) "Our interest is not in changing base metals into gold, the alchemist's dream. Rather, we change rock into useful metals."

While VOICE OVER talks, the Tamers are filling the machine's hopper with rock.

"The Westinghouse Mass Spectrograph has an inside temperature so high that this rock is broken down into individual molecules. It is able to sort through these molecules and collect those of any given element."

(SAFETY NOTE: During this skew the holo team must be careful. Y-axis cameraman must wear thermal armor, as he comes within two meters of the machine's exhaust beam.)

time	origin	skew	X Y Z
151		−082	
152		−081	
153		−080	
154		−079	
155		−078	
156		−077	

HOLD SKEW TO

| 161 | | −077 | 3.5,3.5,2.0 |

FASTER SKEW, SLOW
SQUEEZE & DROP

162		−066	3.3,3.3,1.9
163		−055	3.1,3.1,1.8
164		−044	2,9,2.9,1.7
165		−033	2.7,2.7,1.6
166		−022	2.5,2.5,1.5
167		−011	2.3,2.3,1.4
168		000	2.1,2.1,1.3
169		011	1.9,1.9,1.2
170		022	1.8,1.8,1.1
171		032	1.8,1.8,1.1
172		042	1.8,1.8,1.1
173		052	1.8,1.8,1.1
174		060	1.8,1.8,1.1
175		067	1.7,1.7,1.1
176		073	1.6,1.6,1.1
177		077	1.5,1.5,1.1
178		080	1.4,1.4,1.1
179		081	1.3,1.3,1.1
180		082	1.2,1.2,1.1
181		082	1.1,1.1,1.1
182		082	1.0,1.0,1.1
183		082	0.9,0.9,1.1
184		082	0,8,0.8,1.1

At $t = 156$, one of the Tamers sets the machine's controls.

($t = 156$) "Here, the machine is being set to produce the element silver. (BEAT to $t = 173$) "It will process all that rock in approximately fifteen seconds."

time	origin	skew	X	Y	Z

HOLD THIS
CONFIGURATION TO
187   082   0.8,0.8,1.1

BLUR SQUEEZE
188   082   0.3,0.3,1.1

HOLD THIS
CONFIGURATION TO
197   082   0.3,0.3,1.1

CUT TO:
STOCK AED CUBAGE
44/5398/0329-0345 (Tamer
using lathe on surface of
unimproved planet) FADE TO:
214   HOLD STATIC REPLAY
OF t = 30 TO

219-221   SLOW FADE TO
STOCK AED CUBAGE
79/4760/0000-0008 (Lush
landscape, double sun in sky)

CUT TO:
230
STOCK WEST CUBAGE
PR001/0000-0010
(Westinghouse sigil in front of
deepspace background.
18°/sec. skew.)

232   KEY IN
       WESTINGHOUSE
       ANTHEM
239-240   FADE OUT.

(t = 188) The nugget
appears in the output
hopper.

VOICE OVER: "Silver!
(BEAT to t = 191) "Or any
other useful metal.

"Tamer engineers will use
these metals to build
tools . . ."

(t = 198) "Tools to build
the machines for geoformy.

"And the elements to go
into those machines will also
come from the Westinghouse
. . . Mass Sepctrometer."

(t = 214)   VOICE OVER:

"And given a year or
two . . .

       (DEFIANTLY)
"or ten—or *fifty*—"

(BEAT to t = 221) "There
will be a new world where
men can live.

(BEAT to t = 226) "Another
fresh start for humankind."

(t = 230)   VOICE OVER:

"Westinghouse.

(t = 232)
"Building better worlds . . .

(t = 234)
"For you."

25
Carry the Seed

(From *Sermons from Science* by Theodore Lasky, copyright © 2071, Broome Syndicate. Reprinted from the *Washington Post-Times-Herald-Star-News*, 25 November 2071:)

. . . the original plan, which was to use the LMT to set up automatic geoformy apparatus on one of the terrestrial companions of 61 Cygni A. People would then be transported to the new world by a so-called "generation ship."

Take a cylindrical asteroid about ten kilometers long; hollow it out and geoform the inside. Spin it slowly, end over end, to produce artificial gravity. Give it a propulsion system and aim it at 61 Cygni, with several thousand people aboard. Depending on which design you used (i.e., how much money you could put into the project), the trip could last anywhere from twenty years to a thousand.

Hence the name. Generations, dozens of them, could be born and die along the way.

A woman named Jerry Kovaly made this cumbersome arrangement unnecessary.

Dr. Kovaly was a biologist in charge of the life sciences phase of geoformy on 61 Cygni A, in the late 2030's. (It was she who coined the term "xenasthenia" to describe the sudden weakness and disorientation a Tamer feels back on earth, if he's eaten food grown from another planet's soil, when the alien molecules slingshot out of his body.)

61 Cygni A was an easy planet to geoform; people could walk unprotected on its surface almost from the start. It was the first planet whose native plants proved edible; it was the first planet on which a human child was conceived.

In the course of a routine physical before her fourth jump

to 61 Cygni A, it was discovered that Dr. Kovaly was several weeks pregnant. There was a slight scandal, since her husband earthside was sterile by vasectomy: he sued for and was granted a divorce when Dr. Kovaly declared her intention to go ahead and have the baby (never revealing the father's identity).

She also decided to give birth on 61 Cygni A, partly because her work there was in a crucial stage, partly because the idea of being the mother of the first human born off-planet appealed to her.

The baby, a boy, was born without any complications. A few weeks later Dr. Kovaly's time was up for that jump. She gathered together the three others who had jumped with her, the "black box," and her new son, and they returned to Earth.

At slingshot time, the child disappeared.

It was an alien artifact.

Besides being a terrible shock to Dr. Kovaly—she had been nursing the child at the time—the disappearance was scientifically and philosophically mystifying. Careful of the embryo's health, Dr. Kovaly had not eaten any native food while pregnant, nor drunk any native water. So the molecules that passed into the embryo through her placenta were all Earth-molecules. The baby, made completely of Earth-stuff, should have stayed on Earth.

Dr. Kovaly went back to 61 Cygni A and deliberately got pregnant again. She gave birth on schedule. But this time—in an action some people condemned as heartless—she left the baby outside the black-box radius when she returned to Earth.

And the infant stayed on 61 Cygni A, permanently. The first human to be a bona fide citizen of another planet.

So there was an easy alternative to the generation ship. The AED began recruiting large numbers of women . . .

. . . a policy the AED first characterized with the motto "Carry the Seed." A combination of ribald backlash and sarcastic comment made them drop the motto immediately.

But the policy still stands. The AED recruits three times as many female Tamers as male, and requires that they bear a minimum of two children on two different planets (and two more, if they want to extend their enlistment to "full career" status).

Genetic analysis is one of the most hard-to-pass tests that a potential Tamer must face. Any genetic predisposition toward diseases on the AED blacklist will fail a candidate, no matter how well-qualified he or she may be otherwise. And careful geneologies are kept on all geoformed planets: theoretically, no pairings are allowed between people more closely related than third cousin. This has not yet become a problem, since first-generation citizens of the Worlds are *de facto* employees of AED, intensely loyal, and dependent on the Agency from cradle to grave.

At this writing, there are 7,498 Worlds citizens, mostly first generation (the number is expected to double every decade or so for some time). The oldest is, of course, Primus Kovaly, who at the age of thirty-one has fathered five children. Reportedly he has resisted the temptation to name any of them Secundus.

26
Autobiography 2051

15 Sept 2051.

No entries for two weeks, been busy. Will try to get it all down.

61 Cygni B is an interesting place, more temperate than Earth, mostly forest and ocean. Gus and I made the jump in shirtsleeves with a two-man floater, Gus holding the black box. Considering how peaceful the planet is, we could hardly have landed in a worse situation.

We appeared about a meter over the surface of an ocean, and were immediately dashed by a huge wave. A storm was in progress. Both of us managed to hang on to the floater while it bobbed around in the foam, but it seemed to take forever to get aboard it. Like trying to reboard a capsized canoe.

I did finally get aboard and strapped in. Then I helped Gus up; once he was in the saddle I raised the windshield and we were off. Wanted to get above the storm before locking in on the homing beam. Took a long time because the winds were powerful and unpredictable, but eventually we were in the sunshine and locked in, about 800 kilometers (it turned out) from Starbase.

We flew for almost four hours. Only one sun was up, and we got thoroughly chilled. Occasionally we passed over islands (including one perfectly round atoll), but otherwise there wasn't much to see.

Starbase is a little more than one kilometer inland, built on the bank of a wide slow river, surrounded by a sort of pine forest. Most of the buildings are made of logs and the streets are of crushed shell. A quiet, orderly place except for the children, of which there are thousands. It was early afternoon when we landed, though, and most of the youngsters were napping.

We floated down into a square in the middle of the town, where two people were playing a kind of bowling game. They didn't seem surprised to see us, but pointed out the AED headquarters for us. It was a little cabin on the other side of the square, and the administrator wasn't in (home for lunch and *siesta*). But he'd left a note pegged to the door that told us where our mates were.

The couple in the square sent us off in opposite directions: Gus toward a woman named Hester and me toward Ellen. We tried not to move with unseemly haste.

Ellen was waiting for me with a pot of herb tea and the disconcerting news that she was a little off schedule. According to her morning checkup, we'd have to wait at least eight hours.

We drank the tea and talked for a while. Ellen was in planetary atmospheres, specializing in tertiary weather control (so she could get a job on Earth if she got tired of being a Tamer). This would be her fourth and last child; the AED let her have it on 61 Cygnus B so she could take part in raising her eldest daughter.

I couldn't pronounce her last name, which was African and had a strange "click" in the middle of it (her grandfather was a black American, descended from slaves, who fought in the second Revolution).

She was intelligent and attractive, and under other circumstances I would have enjoyed her company very much. She sensed my agitation, though, and suggested I take a stroll around Starbase: see the sights and come back in the evening.

The pills they give you to prepare for a breeding mission are supposed to maximize sperm count and motility, but as a side effect they induce a powerful and tenacious state of priapism. So being alone with a beautiful woman whom you can't touch is rather unnerving.

I wandered around town for a few hours, plenty of time to see everything. In a nursery playground I saw a little black girl, about six, who might have been Ellen's daughter. I wondered whether they had invented terms for relationships like "the man who is my brother's father but otherwise not related." Stepfather seems inadequate.

Outside of town I inspected the power station and logging camp, then borrowed a boat to row out into the river. Went back to the logging camp and helped a woman saw down a large tree. My time on the planet was costing the AED more than ten dollars a minute; they might as well get some work out of me.

Around dusk I went back into town. This time of year, it never got really dark, because 61 Cygni A came up about the time B set. It didn't provide much heat, but was a good deal brighter than the full moon.

I found the planet's only tavern, a small adjunct to the adults' dining area. It was almost full, with five patrons. One of them was Gus.

He had accomplished his mission, of course. Hester was out on the river, checking crab pots; she was going to meet him here for the night's party (everybody coming to watch us disappear). I started to tell him about my problems with Ellen, but he said he knew. The whole town knew.

The only drink was a strong sour beer that they served with ice, flavored with fruit juice. If you drink it fast enough and are careful to avoid the aroma, it's sort of like a *Berlinerweiss*. We started talking about that, naturally enough in German, and stayed in German when the conversation shifted to women, our four barmates in particular. And that's what started the trouble.

The German was the last straw, anyhow. I haven't felt so edgy since school days, what with the physical discomfort, anxious clockwatching, drugs screwing up my hormones . . . and comparing my wretched state to Gus's obvious comfort. And suspecting that I was the object of a certain amount of ribald speculation by the adults on the planet, ninety percent of whom were female.

Gus has that irritating Germanic habit of constantly correcting your grammar while you're trying to talk, muttering the proper forms sotto voce. It got me rattled; in the course of assembling a complicated sentence I managed to use the wrong mood, and put the primary verb phrase in the wrong place, with the wrong declension.

He laughed.

I slugged him.

He was more startled than injured. I hit him on the shoulder, not too hard, but neither of us was accustomed to three-fourths gravity, and the blow was sufficient to tip his chair back. His Tamer reflexes took over; he twisted out of the chair, made a soft landing on fingertips and toe, and sprung back up.

I got out of my chair to help him, anger gone as quickly as it came. He looked at me in a puzzled way and explained that he hadn't been laughing at my German, which wasn't bad for one so out of practice, but at the unconscious pun I'd made on the verb *schiessen*. I apologized and laughed at the joke and tried to explain my mental state. He understood perfectly, he said, but was distant. I wondered what kind of report he was going to file.

An hour early, Ellen came to the tavern door and signaled me. We hustled back to her cabin. She proved to be a tender and humorous lover. My own performance was remarkable in certain unsettling ways, but she was accustomed to that. She said we would have to get together under more conventional circumstances one day.

And remarked wistfully that two of her three previous mates didn't live long enough to keep their appointments.

Our going-away party was fun, but it was a little strange to be at an affair where most of the people were pregnant women (the seven men who were stationed there semipermanently all wore vasectomy bracelets and a haggard look). The steamed "crabs"—if you can call something with twelve legs a crab—were exotic and delicious, a rare treat for the natives as well as for Gus and me. The children eat them all the time, but the adults have to strictly limit their intake of alien protein. Otherwise the slingshot xenasthenia can be fatal.

At the appointed time we jumped back to Colorado Springs. After a short debriefing we went our separate ways.

There was a note from Carol in my box, saying she had rented a cottage in Nassau for a couple of weeks. I was to call if I didn't want to come; she would find another companion.

There was a Denver-Miami flight leaving the next hour. I managed to get on it, then chartered an aged floater to Nassau. I'd telephoned from Miami, so she was waiting for me at the Paradise Island heliport.

Tamers don't make quite enough to stay on Paradise Island, not by an order of magnitude. We took a jinriksha to the place she'd rented on Nassau proper.

It had been some time since I'd gone anyplace more foreign than Denver, at least on earth. Nassau was full of strange sights and sounds and smells, and it was crowded. God, was it crowded. A half-million people on a tiny speck of land.

I'm as cynical as any Tamer about the highflown rhetoric the AED uses to justify its colonization program. Anyone with basic macroeconomics knows the real story. But the comparison was inevitable between this packed island and the bucolic village I'd left a few hours before. Maybe things will fall apart again; maybe this time will be the last time. One rash person in the right place and the earth could be a sterile cinder in seconds, but that's been more-or-less true for a century.

Still, I was glad that all those babies were up there in the sky. And comforted that one of them would be partly me.

When we got inside the cottage Carol asked whether I had successfully "carried the seed." I told her that it had been very much the other way around—and offered to demonstrate. The effects of the last pill hadn't quite worn off, and I still had two of them left. She thought it sounded interesting.

Two days later I was so exhausted she had to go swimming without me. Mark Twain once wrote to the effect that there wasn't a woman alive who couldn't defeat any ten men at the ultimate battleground between the sexes. When I first read that I thought he was exaggerating. (And I probably would've envied the seven male captives of Starbase.)

We did other things while we were in the Islands: went to a festival, sailed in an ancient windjammer, swam and skindived all the time. Sunned and rested and read some good books. Will write more tomorrow morning. Can't put off this stack of reports any longer.

I was glad to hear that Dr. Jameson lived. Vivian says he claims the bridge made him do it. Maybe it's in this stack somewhere.

27
Touch Me Not

Text of postoperative interview between Dr. Raymond Sweeney (Chief, Psych Group) and Dr. Philip Jameson. 2 September 2051.

(Thirty seconds of introductory politeness)

JAMESON: Are you recording this, Ray?

SWEENEY: What makes you—

J: Come off it, Ray. I'm not being paranoid. We've worked together for over ten years, and I've never seen you wear a coat. You needed it to carry the recorder . . . because one shirt pocket has your cigarettes, and the other—

S: All right, Sherlock, I'm recording. You mind?

J: Why should I? It's like I told the orderly—you talked with the orderly?

S: He didn't understand what you said.

J: You mean he thought it was crazy.

S: Well . . .

J: Sounds crazy to me, too. But it *is* true. I didn't try to commit suicide. That god-damned creature, that bridge, had control of me, made me cut my throat.

S: It did an expert job.

J: (*Fingering scar*) That it did. Right under the ear and then straight across the carotid, deep. Lucky I can talk.

S: The work of a skilled surgeon . . .

J: Bullshit, Sweeney. It obviously had access to my mind. (*Pause*) If I were going to commit suicide, I could do it more successfully, a thousand different ways. Not by opening an artery in a roomful of doctors, next door to a hospital.

S: Phil, most suicides don't want to die. They want to be saved.

J: All right, I know that. But don't you think it's quite a coincidence? With what happened to poor Willard?

S: But Willard didn't attempt suicide; he—

J: Had a heart attack, sure. Path of least resistance.
(*Pause*) The creature tried for my heart, too, Ray. Just before I blanked out, I felt this tightness, squeezing in my chest. But my heart's strong. It was easier for the creature to control my arm.

S: Blanked out?

J: That's right. Just as I went to make the first incision. I felt dizzy and . . . thick, I don't know. Then every thing went white and I woke up being prepped for surgery.
(*Pause*) Have they done an autopsy on Willard?

S: Yes.

J: Well?

S: It was inconclusive. We're having specialists—

J: In other words, his heart stopped and nobody knows why.

S: We have to wait—

J: I rest my case, damn it! Ask your cardiac specialists what sort of heart ailment would cause a robust man to sit down and die quietly in seconds. That thing had control of him. It found the weakest part of his body and squeezed the life out of him.

S: That's awfully dramatic.

J: What happened to me was pretty god-damned dramatic. I was *there*, Sweeney; I felt the thing take over. It just didn't do as good a job on me as it did on Bob. And that first Tamer, the Chinese boy . . . . Has anyone talked to the two Tamers who were in contact when we tried to dissect it?

S: One of them's on a mission. The other said that the bridge functioned normally up to the time when Willard or you touched it. Then it didn't function at all.
(*Pause*) That's what they expected, though. It's never worked with three people.

J: I see. . . . Listen, Sweeney. I'll make a deal with you. You can shrink my head all you want; I'll cooperate a hundred per cent. If you conclude that I have suicidal tendencies, I'll take an indefinite leave of absence.

S: I don't think—

J: *But* . . . in the meantime, I teach you everything I know about invertebrate anatomy. And the next time they bring one of those creatures back . . .

S: I get to cut it up.

J: That's right.

S: Fair enough. Unless you can convince me. I don't think I have suicidal tendencies, either.

28
Chapter Eight

John Thomas Riley usually liked his job: Director of Personnel and Operations Chief for AED, Colorado Springs. Sometimes it was not so pleasant.

He went into the briefing room and the talking stopped abruptly. He sat down at the end of the seminar table and began without preamble.

"I know there's been talk." The ten Tamers stared at him. He wished he'd brought some papers to fiddle with. "People have called this a suicide mission. But it definitely is not."

Three of them nodded, good. "It's pretty well established that the Groombridge bridge killed two people, and almost a third, by telepathic control of their bodies. And we're asking you to go collect as many of the creatures as you can find.

"But this bridge was handled by a total of 38 people, and did no harm to 35 of them. We know that in two out of three cases the creature killed in self-defense. Or attempted to kill. And we aren't asking you to harm them. Lefavre?"

Jacque put down his hand. "That's the main thing that's bothering us. Ch'ing wouldn't have harmed the bridge. Not intentionally, anyhow."

"Maybe there was some kind of accident," Carol said. "He squeezed it too hard, or something."

"We'll never know, of course," Riley said. "But we have to go on the assumption that they can somehow sense when an organism is threatening them, and take action.

"How they could do this is a mystery. Physiologically, they seem barely more sophisticated than a sponge. But there is other compelling evidence that they can do this, besides the violence done to the men who attempted dissecting it. Jeeves, you're preparing a report . . ."

"That's right," Tania said. "I've talked to my team about this, but not Manuel's.

"One clue is in the geophysical analysis. We picked up several fossils that appear to be remnants of large carnivores, aquatic ones. The bridges would be obvious sources of food for these creatures.

"But the only place we found any other form of animal life was in the Crater Sea. Completely isolated from the rest of the ecosystem.

"It could be that the bridges came along after some natural disaster that killed off the planet's animal life. Or the bridges themselves might be that natural disaster: once they evolved their telepathic facility, they proceeded to kill off all of their rivals. They wouldn't have to kill every single individual; just reduce the population density to where there weren't enough mating opportunities for each species to survive. This happened to some species of whales, on Earth in the last century.

"We'll have a clearer picture after this trip, of course."

"It still doesn't explain Ch'ing," Jacque said. "Maybe the creature makes mistakes, kills when it's not really threatened. Maybe it kills at random, to keep in practice."

Carol nodded. "We can theorize forever, but we really don't know anything about it."

"We're inferring from an absence of data," Jacque said. "That's lousy science."

Riley shrugged elaborately. "Would either or both of you like to be taken off the mission?" Which would mean a review board and probably dismissal—then a lifetime of debt, reimbursing the AED for your expensive training.

They shook their heads no.

"Would anybody else? It's just a matter of filling out a couple of forms."

No response.

"Good.

"At any rate, you're not likely to come in contact, in bridge rapport, with any of the bridges you catch. The main thrust of this mission is to bring untouched bridges back to Earth, so that they can be studied under controlled conditions.

"Jameson suggests that we screen the world's population for people with phenomenally high Rhine potential; let them make first contact with the bridges. Sounds like a good idea.

"So we don't *want* you to touch them, not if you can help it. . . . You know that the Groombridge Effect is blocked by certain dielectrics—ceramic quasi-metals, for instance. We've built extensions, waldos, for your suits, made entirely of these ceramics. Hopefully, this is what you'll be using to pick up the bridges."

"Nobody told us about that," Jeeves said.

"We weren't sure we'd have them made in time. Krupp's been working night and day. We do have them now, though; that's why I called this meeting. You and your team are going to go train with them today.

"Team B, Ubico, you're free to go, unless there are questions." There were none. "Team A, questions?" None. He stood up. "Well, then. Go on down to the ready room and get suited up. There's a floater on pad C that'll take you out to a place on the Colorado River; it has the extension waldos and the nets you'll be using. Do it right and you're free until the eleventh."

The apparatus worked well. The two nets were semirigid, articulated so as to conform precisely to the river bottom. It took two people to operate a net, one on each bank. The nets would block off a section of river several kilometers long, and then slowly be brought together. They would trap any floating or swimming object more than a centimeter wide.

In the Colorado they wound up with a swarm of thousands of confused fish. They tested their retrieval waldos by picking a few of the best trout. It took a halfhour to get three fish, but trout are faster and slipperier than the Groombridge bridge. Then they rolled up the nets and had a picnic.

GROOMBRIDGE 1618 MISSION, 11 OCTOBER 2051

A TEAM

PERSONNEL:
1. TAMER 5 TANIA JEEVES. FEMALE, 31. 9TH MISSION. SUPERVISOR.
2. TAMER 3 GUSTAV HASENFEL. MALE, 26. 6TH MISSION.
3. TAMER 2 (PROB) JACQUE LEFAVRE. MALE, 26. 3RD MISSION.
4. TAMER 1 VIVIAN HERRICK. FEMALE, 24. 2ND MISSION.
5. TAMER 1 CAROL WACHAL. FEMALE, 24. 2ND MISSION.

EQUIPMENT:
5 GPEM MODULES W/GROOMBRIDGE 1618 MOD
1 PERSONNEL RECORDER
1 HOMING FLOATER W/GROOMBRIDGE 1618 MOD (SECOND SHOT)
2 SERVO NETS (THIRD SHOT)
1 MASS SPECTROGRAPH, WESTINGHOUSE MOD 17 (FOURTH SHOT)
1 COLLECTING TANK (FOURTH SHOT)

POWER REQUIREMENT:
3 SHOTS 17.89688370924 SU, TUNING @ LOCAL TIME
10:24:38.37677BDK399057
10:32:29.66498BDK399059
10:36:46.00983BDK399060
1 SHOT 17.89688370930 SU, TUNING @ LOCAL TIME
10:42:05.83997BDK399062

MISSION PRIORITY 1.

FUNDING #733092 PSYCH   40%
        #483776 EXOB   20
        #000101 PR   20
        #000100 GENEX   20

They came out of the LMT near Groombridge's southern pole. The floater that followed eight minutes later had been modified to approach and then hover nearby, awaiting Tania's command (to prevent the kind of accident that had left them grounded on the first mission).

They got aboard the floater and homed in on the two nets. That, and taking the nets to the river where they'd found the first bridge, totaled over three hours' flying time. They unloaded and Tania asked for a volunteer.

"The collecting tank and the MS are a couple of hundred kilometers away. Who wants to go get them?" Silence. "Less than a two-hour job."

"We should have arranged for B Team to pick them up," Gus said. "It's really their job."

"Too late to change things now," Jacque said. "Let's draw straws."

Tania had everyone pick a number between one and a hundred. Carol lost.

The other four immediately set up the nets, isolating a kilometer-long stretch of the river. The intent was to surprise a number of the creatures, not allowing one to warn the others away.

Of course, there was always the chance that there had been only one bridge on the planet, and it had sought them out. If so, they would spend forty-seven days in fruitless wading.

Jacque thought they would probably catch dozens, maybe hundreds, on each sweep. Spend most of the seven weeks playing with the mass spectrometer.

The actual results fell somewhere in between. When Carol came back with the floater, they were just about through with the first sweep. It was quite a contrast to their practice session: no activity, just a coalescing mat of floating weed. The nets joined at the bottom and they hauled them in.

After an hour of picking through the mess, they found one bridge.

They hurried downstream fifty kilometers and repeated the process. Nothing. They did it again: nothing again.

On the fourth try they came up with another bridge.

B Team showed up, homed in on the MS, and started mining the mud.

That first day was the only day Tania's team caught two bridges. At the end of the seven weeks they had a total of eight bridges. B Team fared better. They had built a small town of airtight, interconnected A-frame huts: rigid silvery tents of aluminum-silicon alloy. They were in high spirits.

Tania's team was bored and frustrated. Jacque had exploded several times and even snapped at Carol. When they huddled together for the translation back to Earth, it was with desperate relief.

29
They Also Serve

Arnold Bates spends half his life sleeping or taking drugs. Most of the drugs are to help him get to sleep. He is a millionaire several times over, but spends little: rent and food and drugs. He has no hobbies.

When he is awake he is more awake than most people. He must be; he is Senior Controller of the LMT chamber at Colorado Springs. Its 120-centimeter crystal is the largest that AED has, and the busiest.

Bates is a short, wiry man with a shock of white hair framing Amerind features. His skin is pale for an Amerind. He looks fifty but is thirty-two years old. He has been a Controller for ten years, twice the time it normally takes to wear a person down. He has the kind of nerveless self-control that would make an ideal Tamer, but he carries too many bad genes for the job.

His stomach is made of plastic and his liver is a machine. He has an IQ of 189 and gunslinger reflexes.

His main job is to prevent another Los Alamos disaster. Two human bodies trying to occupy the same place at the same time turned a mountain into a deep valley and spread heavy fallout from Albuquerque to Mexico City.

He is looking at the first page of his schedule for today, 27 November 2051:

Jumps	Returns	Slack	Mission	Comments
06:09:14		12:38	τ Ceti	Breeding (3)
	06:26:34	17:20	61 Cyg B	Samples for Agr Grp
	06:36:14	09:40	Procyon A	Tamers (5)
	06:42:45	06:31	Procyon A	Floater
	07:04:59	22:14	70 Ophiuchi A	Tamers (6)
	07:12:33	07:34	70 Ophiuchi A	Floater
07:17:44		05:11	τ Ceti	Food (hurry crew)
	07:35:27	17:43	Groombridge 1618	Tamers (5)
	07:43:18	07:51	Groombridge 1618	Floater
	07:47:37	04:18	Groombridge 1618	Misc equipment
	07:52:56	05:19	Groombridge 1618	Samples for Bio Grp, Psy Grp (both on standby)
	08:04:01	11:05	E Indi	Tamers (5)
		16:38		Training

He will be on today from six to ten AM and from two to six PM. The clock in the controller lounge says 05:58.

The door to the control room opens and a young man steps out. Bates has seen him off and on for almost a year, but doesn't know his name.

"Bates," he nods; Arnold nods back. "It's clear now; you've got better'n ten minutes' slack." Arnold knows this, of course: ten minutes and forty-some seconds. When he opens his eyes in the morning he knows what time it is, to the minute.

The young man is pale, mopping his forehead.

"Trouble?"

"Yeah, bad one last hour. Geoformy team with three injuries, one deader. Slingshot deader."

"Tamers," Arnold says. "Can't learn to keep their arms in."

"Yeah." He shuffles out the door and Arnold goes into the control room. His partner is Mavis Eisenstein, overlapping him on the four-to-eight shift. He's known her for four years.

"Morning, Mavis." She nods and sighs, gets up from the prime chair and moves over to the other one, the backup.

Arnold sits down and opens a fresh pack of cigarettes. He puts that and his old pack on the table in front of him, lights up.

"Wish you were here at five," Mavis says. "Instead of me."

"That's what he said. Real mess?"

She nods, keeps nodding. "One on the bottom cut right down the middle. Even got blood on the glass. Everybody else fell all over. Coordinator and two others were unconscious anyhow. Still don't know what happened."

"Geoformy team?"

"'E Eridani. 05:27:14. Their fucking MS coming in right on top of them, 03:29 slack. Had to steam and bake."

"That's only a two-twenty cycle."

"Don't I know?" Her voice is thin, strained. "Fucking autopsy made me hold. Wanted the cadaver. Almost didn't make it, steamed one of the loading crew, pretty bad I think. Cycled out with nine seconds slack at that."

"Too close. Better file a report."

"Bet your clock I'll file a report. Six," she says, automatically, as double chimes announce the hour. "Fucking autopsy acts like they run the place."

"Want a pill?"

"Took one six minutes ago. I'll be all right."

He checks down through the eleven missions they'll be doing together. "Anybody standing by for the Ag Group samples?"

"No. They called last night, we're supposed to store. Runner coming at nine."

"Tell the loading crew about the squeeze on this food shipment?"

"Oh, yeah. Better call again. I prepared them at four but they maybe brought in some new people after the five-twenty-seven. One for sure."

Arnold places the call. "Whole new crew, as a matter of fact."

"What about the one I steamed?"

"He's alive," Arnold lies instantly. She can find out later. "Fair condition."

"Hated to do that."

"They get paid for it." He points through the window. "There's our breeders."

"Thirty seconds early."

"Twenty-five," he corrects.

The loading crew has already brought out the floater, now standing upright, centered over the LMT crystal. The three Tamers approach it.

Arnold switches his throat mike to broadcast inside the chamber. "Hey, you guys." They wave.

"Don't climb up there yet. Just have to hang on for seven minutes. I'll drop the cylinder in five; that'll give you two minutes fourteen seconds slack. Plenty of exercise."

"Wish they'd do a double shot on these," Mavis says. "Not much volume tolerance."

"Can't do it for Tau Ceti," Arnold says.

"That's right, I forgot. Too much water, big fish."

They wait in silence for a few minutes. Then Arnold tells the breeders to climb aboard and he swings the control keyboard over onto his knees. He rests his fingers lightly on the eight emergency keys: SPILL, FILL, HALF SPILL, HALF FILL, BAKE, STEAM, MEDICAL, KILL MISSION.

There are twenty-four secondary buttons on the three rows underneath. His right forefinger automatically touches the one that used to say DROP CYL. The letters have been worn off the button. The only other secondary whose letters have been worn off is AUTOPSY.

"Why do they have both of us on?" Arnold says. The usual combination is an experienced controller in prime, with a new one in backup.

"The Groombridge thing."

"Ah." The breeders in place, Arnold drops the cylinder. His finger rests lightly on the KILL MISSION button. He doesn't launch the LMT, of course—that requires timing to within a hundred-thousandth of a second—but he can kill the jump if he gets a distress signal from inside the cylinder.

The cylinder rises automatically. "Gone." He swings the keyboard away and looks at her. "What Groombridge thing?"

"Don't you even read the papers?"

"No."

"They found these creatures that let people read minds. Little squirmy—"

"Oh, yeah. I saw on the cube, that doctor. Claimed one of them made him cut his throat."

"That's it. And killed another doctor. They don't understand quite what happened."

Arnold shakes his head. "As if the world wasn't a dangerous enough place already. If they want to play with those things, they ought to go to Groombridge and do it."

"Yeah," Mavis says. "Scientists."

30
Nine Lives

(From *Mindbridge: A Preliminary Evaluation*, Jameson *et al*, AED TFX, Colorado Springs, 2052:)

The first experiments with the Groombridge bridge ended in tragedy; the second series began with tragedy.

The second Groombridge expedition brought back eight untouched bridges. We had assembled twenty-three people who were among the most gifted psychics in the world: their control scores on the standard Rhine tests averaged from 413.7 to 499.9.

This last score belonged to the amazing Jerzy Krzyszkowiak, the only person in history who could reliably perform feats of telekinesis. In our laboratory he was able to exert several grams' pressure on the pan of an evacuated analytical balance, for hours at a time, the balance being out of his sight in an adjacent room.

The twenty-three psychics had chosen seven of their number at random to be privileged with the experience of primary contact (all having agreed that Krzyszkowiak should be among the "lucky" eight). Eight more were chosen for secondary contact.

These sixteen entered the Groombridge chamber at 14:36 on 27th November 2051.

Within seven minutes, half of them were dead.

Every person who experienced primary contact was killed by it. None showed any symptoms of distress until the first died, little more than a minute after touching the bridge. All experimenting stopped while the two attending physicians went to his aid. Then the other primaries died, one by one.

Analyzing the tapes of the tragedy, we found a direct relationship between the individual's psychic ability and the length

Name	Rhine Score	Survival Time
Krzyszkowiak	499.9	01m 17s
Cochran	461.7	02m 28s
Akii-Bua	458.9	02m 35s
Shavlakadze	451.1	03m 00s
Gutterson	440.9	03m 24s
Lindblom	437.3	03m 51s
de Silva	430.9	04m 18s
Hawtrey	413.7	06m 20s

of time he or she survived after primary contact. The accompanying table and graph illustrate this relationship.

The first person ever to make primary contact was the Tamer Hsi Ch'ing, who survived for three hours and forty minutes. If we assume that his Rhine score was 100 (there are no data), then his death agrees with this exponential curve.

Secondary contact proved to have no ill effects, as was also true in the first set of experiments.

Several theories have been advanced to account for this "reflex killing" on the part of the bridges. In the previous section we described the unfortunate demise of Robert Willard, and the bridge's attempt on the life of this author when we tried to dissect the creature prior to its "slingshot" transformation. The reflex in this case is understandable in terms of self-preservation. But it is less easy to explain the reflex killing of primaries, and the obvious relationship between time-lag-to-death and Rhine potential.

A theory first advanced by Hugo Van der Walls takes into account the fossil evidence of . . .

31
Crystal Ball I

No one alive in 2051 will ever understand the Groombridge bridge.

The truth was deduced in 2213 by a woman who happened to be the great-great-great-great-grandniece of Jacque Lefavre (no great coincidence: half the planet was at least that closely related to him). Her name is difficult to translate, since her language was partly telepathic, but it was something like "Still Cloud Yet Changing: Anthropologist."

Still Cloud was investigating some unspectacular ruins left on a planet circling Antares, remnants of an extinct nonhumanoid race that had been studied extensively in the previous generation. These ruins had just been discovered, but Still Cloud studied them for years without any significant findings.

This race worshiped an ugly creature whose name we may translate as God, who supposedly lived inside the planet. An odd feature of their religion was that they believed that every inhabited planet had its own God—yet the race did not have space travel. Nowhere could she find that they had any concrete evidence that life existed on other worlds; it was simply an article of faith.

Eventually Still Cloud uncovered a palace that belonged to the planet's highest religious leader. Underneath the palace was a labyrinthine system of tunnels, one of which led to a chamber, or apartment, that still gleamed with luxury after a quarter of a million years of abandonment: the place where God lived.

What she and other investigators had taken as myth and metaphor was actual fact: their God was an immortal, omnipotent creature who had descended from heaven to live under the earth and rule their lives and destinies. It was the representative of a race that once ruled this corner of the galaxy with benign, but absolute, authority.

In the apartment was a machine that functioned as a library. It was still in good working order; immortals build things to last. In it there was a reference to the star humans called Groombridge 1618, and to the telepathic creatures that lived there.

This immortal race had constructed the Groombridge bridge for its own amusement. It served as a scorekeeper in a decades-long game that involved the precise matching of emotional states. The planet Groombridge had been subjected to a kind of reverse geoformy: its ecology simplified so that none of the indigenous fauna would interfere with the game.

Human scientists were guilty of parochialism in classifying the Groombridge bridge as a physiologically simple creature. It is in fact the most complex organism ever studied—more complex than the scientists who have to dissect it by remote control.

Its true form will never be directly perceived by humans, human senses being limited to three spatial dimensions and the one-way arrow of time. The wiggly nudibranchiform creature that taught humans how to read minds is pure illusion—the simplified projection of a four-dimensional object onto three dimensions. In the same way, the projection of an unabridged dictionary onto two dimensions—its shadow—is identical to the gray rectangle projected by a blank piece of paper, and gives no clue as to the object's complexity.

When this race of Gods decided to destroy itself, it saw no reason to tidy up beforehand. So the Groombridge gameboard remained for future, simpler, races to puzzle over.

The planet that Still Cloud studied had been dead and cold for two hundred millenia when the Gods went home to die. Home was a couple of thousand light years away, which distance they traveled instantaneously, by an application of will.

In Jacque Lefavre's time, all that was left of the home of the Gods was a rapidly expanding nonthermal radio source called the Cygnus loop.

The light of Their passing had enabled Neanderthal men to hunt at night for several months.

32
Help Wanted

An advertisement appearing in every major newspaper in Nevada the week of March 4-11, 2052:

DIE
FOR
MONEY

WANTED: LEGAL SUICIDES

IF you have a legal suicide permit, and can supply proof of good health and mental stability, we offer you the chance to make a unique contribution to science while leaving a sizable sum to your heirs.

PROJECT THANOS will pay up to $10,000 for qualified subjects. Amount paid will depend on the subject's score on a battery of psychological tests. Minimum pay will be $2,500.

If interested, please write or call:

PROJECT THANOS
Box 7777
Colorado Springs
Colorado 7019464

3037-544-2063, Extension 777

33
Chapter Nine

The next two years were full ones for Jacque and Carol. Together they did a couple of months' dog-work geoformy on Procyon A, then spent six months on Earth as subjects in an intensive research project on the Groombridge bridge. They duplicated their experiment of 26 August 2051, this time with more symmetrical results.

They were getting used to living together, and talking about someday getting a contract, when Carol was tapped for her first breeding mission. Jacque applied to be father, a request which might normally be granted, but unfortunately the planet was 61 Cygnus B. AED policy on this was inflexible: no man was allowed to contribute more than .05% of a planet's genetic pool (women were allowed .2%) in the first and second generations.

During the nine months Carol was working and getting round on 61 Cygnus B, they saw each other only once, even though she spent four of those months on Earth to minimize xenasthenia.

Jacque had shown an unusual sensitivity to the Groombridge bridge, so when the project was moved to the smaller crystal at Charleville, Australia, he went along. He shuttled back and forth several times between Charleville and Groombridge (one place as bleak as the other, he claimed), making secondary contact with bridges after the volunteer suicides touched them first.

It wasn't pleasant, being in bridge rapport with someone who knew he was going to die. Some of them looked forward to it. Some had second thoughts. One tried to speed up the process by running into the exhaust beam of a mass spectrograph. With a GPEM suit, nothing would have happened to him. With the minimal protection they wore on Groombridge, he lived almost an hour.

Carol had a smooth delivery and the AED gave her and
Jacque six weeks' leave together. They had saved up a lot of
salary, with nothing to spend it on, and decided to blow it all in
Africa and Europe.

Paris was a little cool in late October, 2052, but Jacque was
determined. He'd found a cafe on the Left Bank whose pro-
prietor had set a few tables out on the sidewalk, hoping to snag
a crazy tourist. Jacque pulled his collar up and poured a few
more drops of water into his Pernod. When he'd been here as a
little boy, you could still see the Seine, even here, across from
the Louvre. Now it was wall-to-wall houseboats. It was also,
the guidebooks said, an unhealthy place for tourists to be, after
dark. But Jacque was protected by his Tamer uniform. Not only
were Tamers supposed to be tough, but if you hurt one the AED
would have you in a soft room for the rest of your life.

The caller worked into his belt buckle sounded three short
zips: signal to call Colorado Springs. He'd been called a dozen
times in France; various people were going over his Charleville
report. They usually called around dinner time.

He carried his drink into the cafe and got the bartender's
attention. *"Où se trouve le téléphone?"*

The bartender reached under the bar and produced an
ancient handset, with a screen instead of a cube, and asked
whether it was a local call. Jacque said no, but collect. He
nodded and unlocked it. Jacque punched up 3037-544-2063.

The switchboard plugged him into Operations, but he got a
holding pattern with a SECURITY DAMPER message. This
antique didn't have a sight-and-sound focus, so he compromised
by carrying it into the farthest corner before thumbing the COM-
MENCE button.

The message snapped off and John Riley's face appeared.
It wasn't routine, then. Jacque had a sinking feeling that his
vacation was over.

"This is a recording," Riley said.

"All Earthbased Tamers are recalled to Colorado Springs.

Immediately. This is the single most important thing that has ever happened to the Agency. And that is putting it very mildly.

"Stay on the line. If you're calling long distance, you'll be switched to the transportation operator. Otherwise—be here as soon as possible. Main amphitheater."

Riley faded and was replaced by Mike Sohne, a drinking buddy of Jacque's, who looked harried.

"Mike! What's up?"

Half-second lag; satellite relay. "Oh. Hi, Jacque. Don't know, guess I'll find out when you do. The place is in an uproar, everybody running around and nobody talking. We had a long-range probe come back all deaders, that's all I know. Don't even know that for sure. . . . You're in Paris?"

"That's right."

"Lucky son of a bitch. Look, you have to be here by 1300. That's 2000 Greenwich, 2100 your time."

"Two hours?" Jacque checked his watch. "You've—"

"That's right. One hour fifty minutes."

"You'll have to start without me, then. End without me, too. I can't get a flight out—"

"Uh-uh, Jacque. Just get your ass over to Orly. Is Wachal with you?"

"No, she's out shopping somewhere."

"I mean is she in Paris."

"Oh, sure. I just don't know—"

"She must've got one of the other operators, then. Get over to Orly as fast as you can and wait for her. Or she'll wait for you. You're reserved on pad thirty-nine, that's a suborbital express."

"But Mike, look . . . all of my stuff is back at the hotel— my fucking *pass*port! I can't—

"Don't worry about it, we'll clean up after you. I punched up the travel budget here and got all nines. What hotel?"

"Uh . . . Studio Etoile, just a second." He pulled a matchbook out of his pocket. "That's 32-754-69-31, got it?"

"Okay. Passport. . . . You don't know your number?"

"No."

"No matter, I'll give them a picture. When you get to Orly, go to the departures wing and find out who's in charge."

"All right."

"See you in a couple of hours. Endit."

"Endit," Jacque said to the empty screen.

Jacque and Carol were sitting in the amphitheater in Colorado Springs. "Oh, did you find that dress you wanted?"

"Suit, not dress. No, the ones I liked cost too much. If I'd known we were coming back today I would've bought one."

"Yeah." There were four or five hundred people in the hall, murmuring. "I would've drunk faster."

"You drank fast enough. You still smell like a licorice factory."

"Love it." A woman came out on the stage and set up a podium. "Feeling better?"

"No." She was taking hormones to suppress lactation. She was dizzy and her breasts ached. "Free fall didn't help."

A shimmering cube appeared around the podium. A white blob in the center shrank to a sharp point, and the cube disappeared: holo projectors focused. John Riley came out and put a couple of sheets of paper on the podium. The crowd fell silent.

He looked around. "I don't know exactly where to begin." He tapped the podium nervously. "This all started with the astrophysics group. Some fellows from Bellcomm University came to them with a jump proposal. To Achernar."

Somebody whistled. "That's right, 115 light-years. Expensive proposition. Bellcomm offered to match funds, but we haggled and . . . they wound up paying ninety percent.

"Well, it seemed reasonable. No way we could colonize a planet that far away. Besides, it's a B5 star, not likely to have anything interesting.

"The Bellcomm people, Drs. Wiley and Eisberg, had been

mapping gravity waves. They caught a strong pulse from Achernar. Looking back over the records, they found similar pulses occurring for over twenty years, at irregular intervals.

"You're all familiar with the normal mechanisms that produce gravity waves. There's nothing about Achernar that suggests it could be a source. So they wanted to go take a look.

"We tapped Shirley O'Brien's team for this, a thirty-minute jump. Outfitted them as we would a normal trailbreaker assignment, plus some gadgets the Bellcomm people gave them. This is what came back."

The auditorium lights dimmed and the podium and Riley disappeared, replaced by an image of the LMT chamber. Nothing happened for a few seconds. Then half a GPEM suit appeared. It toppled over and spilled. Collective gasp of anguish.

The lights returned; Riley was wiping his forehead with a handkerchief. "All right, it's not very pretty. But it's the chance we all take, every time we step on to that crystal.

"That's what we thought it was, just a horrible slingshot accident. Evidently O'Brien had gotten separated from her team, and had the black box off-center when return time came up. How they could manage to get separated on a thirty-minute jump we didn't know.

"Her personnel recorder was intact, though, and she was carrying an automatic holo camera for Bellcomm. So we could find out what happened.

He paused and shook his head. "I won't keep you in suspense," he said quietly. "What they found was an anomalous Earthlike planet. An inhabited planet.

"Quiet, please. The people, the creatures, on this planet were evidently not indigenous. They seemed also to be an exploration team. And they found O'Brien, not vice versa.

"They landed on nightside and waited for their floater." Riley nodded at the projectionist.

The Tamers were standing in a broad savannah in dim blue moonlight. There were dark mountains on the horizon, and large single trees every couple of hundred meters. They were talking excitedly. O'Brien had just relayed the information that the planet had a terrestrial atmosphere.

They were taking soil and plant samples when the floater came. They started to get on board; race to where Achernar was visible before their half hour ran out.

Then another floater landed.

It was a round platform enclosed by a railing, inside a semi-transparent dome. The dome disappeared when it touched the ground.

There were four human beings on the platform; two very female and two very male, wearing nothing but dark tan skin and silver belts. They were beautiful.

They hopped lightly out of their floater and approached O'Brien's team. The woman leading them raised her right hand in a gesture that seemed to mean "wait." Or perhaps a sign of peaceful intent. Then the sky fell.

Between them and the mountains a huge black mass settled noiselessly. In the dim light, no details were visible, only a slender ellipsoid about three kilometers long by a half kilometer wide. A spaceship.

O'Brien had found her voice. "Don't do anything that might seem aggressive. We must look pretty fearsome in the suits."

A seam opened in the front of the ship and warm yellow light poured out. The woman beckoned them toward the light.

"Should we go with her?" one of the crew said.

"It—I don't know," O'Brien said. "Yes. But everybody stay close to me. We jump in twenty-one minutes."

She led them to a ramp that had slid out of the opening in the ship. The Tamers waited while the aliens went up the ramp, which had no apparent moving part but acted like a conveyor belt, and then followed them up.

The ramp was at one end of a corridor that appeared to extend the full length of the ship. Its walls were a seamless, glassy substance that radiated a uniform, soft yellow light.

When the last of them stepped off the ramp, the floor closed behind him. Then there was a hollow "boom," perhaps the ramp sliding back into place.

"Looks like we've been kidnapped," someone said.

"Or collected," O'Brien said. "No matter. The ceiling is high enough for us to pyramid. I don't imagine they could stop us."

The alien leader made half-fists of her hands and put them together over her sternum, then drew them apart slowly: a gesture probably inviting them to open their suits. She repeated it several times, then smoothed a hand over her naked body and smiled. She had too many canines.

"I'll be glad to get out of my suit," a male voice said, "if you promise not to open your mouth."

"Shut up, Jerry. Let me answer." Since the cameras were on her suit, it was impossible to see what O'Brien did. The alien shook her head and said something in a surprisingly low growl.

"That could mean either yes or no, even on Earth."

One of the males rapped on the wall with his knuckles and a small rectangle opened. He reached in with both arms and came out with four objects that looked like old-fashioned microphones. A short length of silvery wire dangled from each.

He handed one to the leader and then to the other two. Each one plugged the wire into his silver belt.

"Couldn't be a translator," Jerry's voice said. "A weapon?"

"Maybe it is a translator," someone said. "We don't know everything. . . ." The leader approached the nearest Tamer, pointed the microphone at him and smiled.

The sound from the holo cube screamed a split second before the audience did.

The beam from a ten-megawatt laser couldn't penetrate that suit, but where she pointed the wand a round hole opened, then widened into a long gash that sprayed blood. Dying, the Tamer snatched her arm and pulled. She dropped the wand as the amplified grip broke her arm.

The other three aliens attacked simultaneously; it was over

in a second. The holo picture tilted sideways, then dimmed red and turned two-dimensional as blood washed over two of the three lenses.

The aliens walked slowly down the corridor, the injured one showing no sign of pain, even though jagged gray bone protruded through the bloodslick on her useless arm. A couple of dozen paces down, the wall opened and they turned left.

The auditorium lights went on. "That's all," Riley said. "There's another nineteen minutes of the same scene. The aliens never come back."

He referred to his notes for the first time. "We—myself and representatives from Bio, Psych, and Senior Survey—we have some tentative remarks, observations about these aliens.

"The most striking thing, of course, is that they look so much like us. The compelling explanation is that we have common ancestors, either in prehistory or . . . well, any number of interesting scenarios. Another possibility is that they are able to change shape, and adapted this form to throw our Tamers off their guard.

"How they could know what a human being looks like is anybody's guess. Perhaps they could read the Tamers' minds.

"That they should conform to our current standards of beauty is a suspicious coincidence. As Dr. Sweeney pointed out, a culture will generally regard as beautiful such characteristics as have survival value, for the individual or for the race. A similar aesthetic about the body presupposes a similar environment. Of course, two highly developed technological societies will have have similar environments, the most comfortable possible. Which brings us back to square one."

He held up a piece of paper. "See whether any of you can add to this list. Dr. Jameson made it up: anatomical differences between us and them.

"The teeth are obvious. But that could be cosmetic; various Earth cultures have filed or chipped teeth to make them look more ferocious.

"Did you notice that the men have no nipples? I didn't. Jameson says they could have been excised in infancy, though, for cosmetic or ritual reasons, and not leave scars visible from our range.

"Their umbilici are all the same, a simple vertical groove. You would almost never find this in four humans chosen at random. The same with genital size in the men. But we have no reason to presuppose randomness; maybe only men with strange navels and large genitalia are recruited for the job.

"Also, the females . . . the genital slit extends about a centimeter higher than it normally does in humans, viewed frontally. And in a low dorsal presentation, the last view we have of the injured alien, the external genitalia aren't visible. They would be in a human."

He shook his head. "These are small details, but maybe one of them is a clue.

"None of the aliens had a mole, birthmark, or other visible skin deformity. Every one of them had brown eyes. The two women were the same height, 173 centimeters. The men were four and seven centimeters taller. Neither of the men ever opened their mouths. All four had long, graceful fingers and the high foreheads that we unconsciously, erroneously, associate with intellectual ability.

"Their fingernails and toenails were closely trimmed, what would be painfully close for a human. Collarbones and shoulderblades less prominent than the average human

"Dr. Jameson feels that the skeletal structure in the legs and pelvis is slightly different than in humans. But that awaits more precise measurement.

"Finally, the injury the female alien sustained. Most people would go into shock and pass out with that kind of a severe fracture. A human might ignore such an injury if he were in a berserker rage, or under deep hypnosis or anesthesia. She seemed to act the same, before and after.

Also, in my opinion, the damage should have been more

severe. He grabbed her just above the elbow, in a dying spasm, and shook her twice. With the GPEM's amplification circuits, that's like being attacked by a bulldozer. Her arm should have come off.

"We'll be running this cube continuously for several days, in Studio A next door. I want everybody to see it over and over, as often as you can stand it. There's no specialty that applies to this problem; there's none that doesn't apply. Anything you come up with, send it on to me through Planning.

"Obviously we have to go back. Probably an automated probe; I won't order anybody to undertake a suicide mission.

"Damned expensive, too. The energy we have to push through the crystal for a 115 light-year jump, just for a couple of hours, would pay for hundreds of routine resupply missions."

He folded the papers together and gave them a sharp crease. "But once we show this cube around, I doubt we'll have any trouble getting funded."

34
Numbers and Dollars

(From *AED Employees' Handbook*, AED TFX, Colorado, 2053:)

It might seem inefficient for us to proceed with geoformy in a sequence of many short jumps, rather than fewer long ones. It is unavoidable, though, from the mathematics of the Levant-Meyer Translation.

To appreciate this, it's not necessary to have a complete technical description of the LMT; indeed, not one in a thousand AED employees understands all of the subtleties of the process. But it's instructive to compare the energy requirements of the crystal for jumps of different duration.

(Readers without first-year college mathematics may wish to skip to the last table.)

The basic equation describing the energy needed for a given jump is:

$$E = C\,\frac{e^{t/k}\cosh s^{1/2}}{(1/t) + 1}, \quad \begin{cases} t \geqq .01356 \\ s \geqq 9.4095 \end{cases}$$

where C and k are constants, t is the duration of the jump, and s is the distance. Calculations are normally done in the MKS system, but for clarity we will consider t in units of days, and s in units of light-years.

The constraints braced to the right of the equation are due to an energy threshold phenomenon of the LMT crystal. Jumps cannot be made to destinations closer than 9.4095 light-years, nor may a jump be of less than about 19½ minutes duration. The first constraint keeps us from exploiting the promising α Centauri system.[1] The second makes it impossible to explore planets more than about 100-light-years distant.

---

[1] There are plans, however, for the τ Ceti colony to build an LMT facility out of native materials, for jumps to α Centauri.

It's a convenient fiction to consider this equation as continuous over the range of values allowed. The LMT, however, can't translate an object to any desired point in space; it translates only from matter boundary to matter boundary. There has to be an object with a distinct and relatively cold surface —a planet or asteroid—"near" the point to which the LMT crystal is tuned (attempts to translate probes onto the surface of planetless stars have always failed). The margin of error allowed is described by a fourth-order differential equation involving distance, energy, and the angular displacement of charge application away from the lattice axis of the LMT crystal.[2]

This family of curves shows the relationship between energy requirement and jump duration for representative distances:

[2] As described in the monograph *Mathematics of the Levant-Meyer Translation: State of the Art 2051*, by Lewis Chandler, AED TFX, Colorado, 2051.

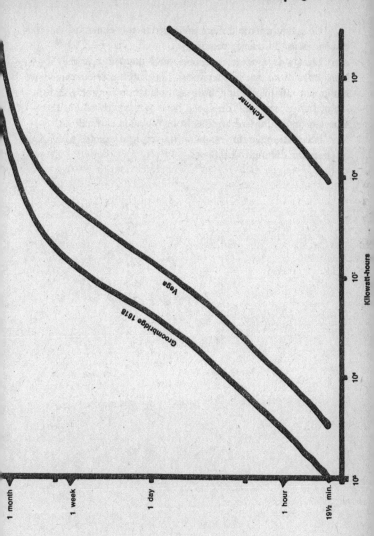

Note that a tenfold increase in distance becomes a thousand-fold increase in energy required.

Energy is money, of course, and the AED is the largest consumer of energy in the world. Like any other consumer, we pay a flat rate to Westinghouse Interplanetary for every kilowatt-hour, though our rate is reduced both because of volume and because of mutual-interest grants from WI research facilities.

It's instructive to compare the cost of jumps to various planets for different durations:

NAME	DISTANCE (L.Y.)	DURATION OF JUMP (DAYS)						
		0.02	0.1	1.0	5.0	10	30	70
Ross 248 [1]	10.3	0.48	2.24	13.6	34.7	64.8	589.0	43,301.4
61 Cygnus A	11.2	0.55	2.58	15.6	39.9	74.3	675.3	49,654.5
Groombridge 1618 [2]	15.0	0.93	4.37	26.5	67.7	126.0	1,145.2	84,200.0
Vega	26.0	3.17	14.86	89.9	229.9	428.3	3,891.0	286,000
Achernar [3]	115	87.97	4,113.82	24,913	63,717	119,000	1,079,000	52,440,000
Canopus [4]	240	10,354	484,200	2,932,000	7,499,000	13,970,000	127,000,000	9,330,000,000

FIGURES REPRESENT COST IN THOUSANDS OF DOLLARS (stab)

[1] The closest star for which the Levant-Meyer Translation is effective.

[2] Planet where the "Groombridge Bridge" was discovered.

[3] At this writing, a short expedition to Achernar is being prepared.

[4] Illustrative only; there has never been a jump to Canopus, and probably never will be. The energy required for the seventy-day jump (if we had a way to produce and store it) would supply all of the Earth's current needs for ten thousand years.

Careful study of this table will give one an appreciation for the complexity involved in scheduling jumps (coordinating them so the crystal is always clear when a return is due).

As an illustrative example, consider the course of a breeding mission to Cygnus A. A pregnant Tamer will spend about 150 days of her pregnancy offplanet. The energy cost of various combinations of jumps is as follows:

$$
\begin{array}{rll}
150 & \text{one-day jumps} = \$2,340,000 \\
30 & \text{5-day jumps} = 1,197,000 \\
15 & \text{10-day jumps} = 1,114,500 \\
5 & \text{30-day jumps} = 3,376,500.
\end{array}
$$

So a sequence of short jumps may actually cost more than a smaller number of longer jumps. What happens in practice is that the least expensive combination is calculated, and then adjustments are made to the sequence in order to minimize crowding of the crystal's schedule . . .

35
Autobiography 2053

Box 5397
Oswego, NY 1312659
3 January 2053

Dear Carol,

It looks like I'll be here for another week. Not looking forward to it, either.

My stepmother insisted on a viewing, open coffin. Barbaric. She said Dad would have wanted it that way. Maybe he changed a lot these last nine years.

The reason I have to stick around is that Dad willed his papers to Cornell, and their history of science department is anxious to have them. He left a trailerful, in no particular order; I'm filing and cataloging them with the help of half-brother Jerry.

Jerry's all right. I never really got to talk with him before. He's just finishing a master's in holo arts. Dad was disappointed he didn't go into physics. Still, he left him everything—all the money, that is. (The house and such went to Zara, my step-mother.) Neither my mother nor I was mentioned in the will.

I called Mother, but she didn't want to come to the funeral. She confronted Zara once. She agreed that Dad wouldn't have wanted all this morbid circus. The will didn't say anything one way or another.

I saw in the *Times* that they think the Achernar gravity waves were caused by interstellar space ships braking. So they've been on that planet for 140 years or more.

The article didn't say, but I assume the gravity waves are generated by a sudden loss of mass as the ships come down from relativistic velocity. They must stop pretty suddenly. Has anybody figured out the gee-forces involved? Tough customers.

At least they don't have the LMT, not yet. After seeing that cube (a hundred times) I'm just as happy we don't have them in our back yard.

I called Noad (Planning) and he gave me a leave extension. They do need a scientist-type here for the sorting. Jerry's smart but he doesn't know a quark from a quasar.

I may come back to Colorado Springs by way of Kuala Lumpur, spend a day with my mother. She remarried three or four years ago, and I've never met the man.

They've been busy years, though.

This letter probably comes as a surprise (pleasant, I hope) since I have been calling every night. Guess I got in the habit of writing when I was in Australia and you were making babies for the greater glory of etc.

I do miss you so much. Take care.

Love,

Jacque

36
Things That Go
Bump in the Night

12 Jan 53

TO: All personnel involved in Project Bogeyman.
FROM: Psych Group (R. Sweeney, chmn).
RE: Psychological profile of the Achernar aliens.

I'm stuffing this in your mailboxes because we just don't have enough to make it worth calling a general meeting.

Take the following list with a ton of salt. The essence of psychology, in the only sense that's applicable here, is in figuring out consistent stimulus-response patterns in the population under scrutiny. We have only a small set of stimuli to consider, and responses that as often as not make no sense whatsoever.

Possible Characteristics

1. Courage or lack of concern over personal welfare.

As O'Brien remarked on the cube, a Tamer in a GPEM suit is a pretty dangerous organism, and looks it. The aliens didn't bother with weapons when they first confronted the five Tamers. Either they didn't realize that the suited Tamers could do them harm—an unlikely supposition in light of their technological sophistication—or they didn't care what happened to them personally (this theory is buttressed by the passive reaction of the female leader to her grave injury).

Another explanation would be a kind of judgmental blindness, an egotism that wouldn't allow them to consider another race as being a potential danger.

2. Confidence; lack of xenophobia.

The female leader was immediately in charge of the situation. She communicated very well in sign language and, again, showed no sign of fear.

3. Aggression.

It would have been interesting to see what the aliens would have done had the Tamers not gone along with them. As it is, all we have to go on is the explosion of violence at the end, and the sound the leader made before the slaughter, which resembled a growl. This could be the normal tone and timbre of their language, though.

4. Sensuality(?).

One gesture the female leader made would have been frankly sexual in a human being. It's more likely, though, that she was simply indicating that the Tamers didn't need their suits inside the ship. (Though it may be worthwhile to remember that human societies allowing casual, nonsexual, nudity do have restrictions on the range of gestures allowed in public.)

5. Incuriosity.

The aliens seemed not at all interested in the Tamers once they were killed. It is possible that something in their philosophy or psychology prohibited them from investigating the dead. As a wild guess, one might posit a purification ritual that had to follow killing; there was no way for them to know that the corpses would soon disappear.

Other Points

1. Smiles.

Although two of the aliens smiled frequently, there is no reason to believe that they were trying to convey a feeling of friendliness, to put the Tamers off their guard. Even in human cultures the smile is often an ambiguous or even negative expression. In other primates, the baring of teeth is usually an aggressive challenge.

2. Tools or puppets.

Dr. Bondi suggests that the aliens O'Brien encountered might not have been the "true" aliens, the ones who built the starship. They may have been constructs, flesh-and-blood robots designed for dangerous work.

This is an ominous possibility, in view of their striking similarity to human beings. The aliens appeared less than five minutes after the Tamers translated onto the planet. If they were puppets constructed to mimic human form, then either their masters were able to divine an accurate picture of human anatomy and build four humans in minutes, or they were already familiar with the human form. It's hard to say which explanation is more frightening. If the first is true, we are dealing with a race that has vast psychic and scientific powers (and apparently no respect for life). If the second, we are dealing with a race that has observed humanity, and presumably knows where Earth is.

3. The aliens as adversaries.

We assume that the aliens have not settled any planets closer than Achernar, since we haven't recorded the peculiar gravity wave bursts in the neighborhood of any closer stars. This doesn't mean they aren't on their way.

In day-to-day work with the Levant-Meyer Translation, we tend to forget, or ignore, the fact that the LMT is a time machine. When we detect a gravity wave from Achernar, it is the record of an event that occurred 115 years ago. If we respond to that event with the LMT, it gathers information 115 years in that event's future; then brings it back to the past for us to investigate.

So if the aliens learned the location of Earth from O'Brien's team (of course, there's no reason to assume that they did), and immediately mounted an expedition to our planet, we would have over a century to prepare for meeting them.

On the other hand, they could have *left* Achernar over a century ago, and be right on our doorstep at this moment.

From a statistical point of view, this fear might seem irrational: there are some twenty thousand stars within 115 light years of Achernar, so why should they single us out?

The answer is that they might be able to detect our civilization. A powerful enough radio receiver in the region of Achernar would at this moment be picking up radio broadcasts that originated on Earth in 1938: undeniable proof of a technological civilization. It's true that the signals would be weak—we have no radio telescopes, in fact, sensitive enough to detect such a signal. But neither have we mile-long spaceships that travel close to the speed of light.

From what little we know about their behavior and capabilities, it's impossible to say how great a threat the aliens actually present. But certainly the only prudent course of action is for the Agency to invest all available money and manpower in learning as much as we can about them, as fast as we can.

(On Tuesday, 14 Jan, there will be a meeting of the Psych and PR groups, along with Planning and the Industrial Relations Committee, to discuss funding for Project Bogeyman. All interested personnel are urged to attend. Auditorium B, 13:30.)

37
Chapter Ten

Jacque and Carol gave the funding meeting a miss. But the next morning a predawn call summoned them to Auditorium B anyhow: emergency meeting, no details. With minimal ablutions, no breakfast, and hasty dressing, it still took them forty-five minutes to get to the auditorium. It was almost filled; they took seats in the back.

"Oh shit," Jacque said as they sat down. "That doesn't look good."

The only thing on the stage was a goldfish bowl filled with slips of paper. Carol nodded. "It probably isn't going to be a raffle."

John Riley got up from the front row and mounted the stage. In an effort to seem causal, he half-sat (stiffly) on the table that held the goldfish bowl.

"Sorry to haul you out of bed like this. It's important.

"The physics group got in contact with me around midnight. They've found out what the aliens' weapon is, and have a way to neutralize it.

"Quiet, please, quiet. . . . It's not really good news, not in the long run."

Dead silence. "Those little, uh, microphone-like things are miniature LMT crystals.

"Yes, I know. . . . Please . . . quiet. . . . Thank you. It seems odd that they would use starships, however fast, knowing about the Levant-Meyer Translation. Makes you wonder.

"Maybe the amount of time a voyage takes doesn't mean anything to them. Or it might just be possible that they've never experimented with large crystals. That they think of it as a . . . sort of a temporary disintegrating ray. Dr. Sweeney's report notes that they may lack scientific curiosity. This doesn't have to be inconsistent with a high level of technology; they could be the decadent descendants of a more vigorous culture, using leftover gadgets that they don't really understand.

"We can hope that it's something like that. It would be unpleasant to have them cropping up on our planets. On earth."

With his finger he stirred the slips of paper in the bowl. "As all of you must know, the LMT field can be deflected up to ninety degrees by a sufficiently strong magnetic field. It's a simple matter to modify a GPEM suit so that it acts as a large magnet. Simple in principle, anyhow. The engineering and bioengineering people will start work on it today.

"We have to get one of those creatures back here for inspection. We have to know what we're up against. Somebody has to go get us one."

He got up and paced two steps, then sat down again. "The last time we were in this room together I told you I wouldn't ask anybody to volunteer for a suicide mission. Well, this isn't exactly . . . that. Still, it's the most dangerous mission any Tamer has ever been asked to do, forewarned.

"What we'll do is send one Tamer to Achernar on a 19½-minute jump. Assuming the aliens show up again, what he has to do is stay with them, near them, until slingshot time. Then grab one. Embrace him and bring him back.

"Obviously a perilous mission. We don't know what other sort of weapons the aliens might have."

He picked up the goldfish bowl and swirled it. "In here, we have the names of every available Tamer, except for pregnant women. That's not out of chivalry; the magnetic field won't be strong enough to harm an adult, but we don't know what it could do to a developing fetus."

"Quick," Carol whispered, "make me pregnant."

"Here?"

"Any one of you is qualified for this mission," Riley was saying. "For my own peace of mind, if nothing else, I don't want a volunteer. Is there any objection to this procedure?"

"Yeah—my name's in that goddamn bowl," Jacque murmured.

Riley picked a Tamer from the front row to draw a name from the bowl and hand it to him.

He looked up. "Wachal. Tamer Three Carol Wachal."

Jacque went with Carol to the Krupp factory in Denver, where GPEM suits were made. She was to get a final fitting and practice using some of the suit's unique accessories.

It was larger than a regular suit and had a shiny, crinkly surface, like rumpled aluminum foil. The man who showed it to them was a Spaniard named Tueme. Jacque had expected a German. He had nothing against Germans, but they always seemed to fall into his life at times of crisis.

"You probably will not have to use all of these things," Tueme said. "But you should test them, and yourself, just in case."

He ran his finger along six metal eggs attached to the suit's chest. "These are limited-radius fragmentation grenades. Each contains thousands of needle-sharp crystals, under pressure, of some sulfur compound that evaporates in air. They will shred any person standing within 2½ meters when they detonate. Beyond 2½ meters, the crystals will have evaporated and will do no harm. They explode on contact.

"We suggest that you try to stay outside of the fatal radius. The crystals will not penetrate your suit, of course, but they might harm your equipment."

"No holo cameras," Carol said.

"No. The Z-axis camera has to be mounted on a boom. It is awkward. There are two flat cameras, front and back.

"Built into the helmet is a ten-megawatt laser which you aim automatically. There are crosshairs on the screen of your image amplifier. Simply look at your target and depress the tongue switch that normally would put you in contact with your unit's supervisor. One-second burst, each time you switch—but use it with caution. It drains power from the magnetic field generator, and will leave you temporarily vulnerable.

"The other tongue switch, that normally calls the food and water tubes, will trigger a strong injection of para-amphetamine: this will accelerate your muscular responses and make your senses temporarily more acute. But it will also affect your judgment; it will make you self-confident, perhaps to the point of recklessness. So use it only in an extreme emergency.

"If you hit the switch a second time, it will deliver a compensating dosage of a depressant. Then you may repeat the para-amphetamine if it is needed again."

"What, no cyanide pill?" Jacque said.

"No, it is not necessary."

"That's good to hear."

"If the aliens overpower you and attempt to open the suit, its power plant will overload and detonate. This will cause a fusion reaction on the order of one megaton."

"I see," Carol said.

"A natural precaution. One that should not be necessary, however. You have many defenses.

"These three bulbs contain a powerful tranquilizing gas." They were rounded cylinders, juice-can-sized, colored yellow green, and red. "The green one is ten times as strong as the yellow. The red, ten times as strong as the green. Be sure to set them off in the proper order. The gas will work on any mammal and many other creatures: the yellow will make a human drowsy and confused; the green will put him to sleep. The red would kill him.

"Just pull the pin on the top and drop the bulb. It diffuses very rapidly, and is effective out to ten or twenty meters."

They fitted Carol to the suit and took her to a "proving ground" (a domed-over vacant lot behind the Krupp factory) where she practiced for an hour on dummy targets. Then she and Jacque had a leisurely dinner at La Fondita and flew with the suit back to Colorado Springs.

The Colorado Spring LMT chamber had never been so crowded. Four Tamers in GPEM suits, one in each quadrant, crouched behind tripod-mounted lasers. Four others had rifles with tranquilizer darts. The walls were lined with specialists, sitting behind stacked sandbags, breathers dangling around their necks. A stubby one-person floater was perched on the crystal, Carol standing beside it in her glittering suit.

Jacque sat waiting on the sandbags. Forty seconds after Carol jumped, a slingshot was coming from Groombridge: volunteer suicide with a fresh bridge. Jacque was to hold the bridge and try to make contact with the alien Carol was bringing back.

If she came back. Jacque had been on mood elevators for two days, a prescription to exorcise black despair. He felt vaguely guilty at not being able to worry about Carol for more than a few minutes at a time.

(They had sent him to the head doctor after he'd exploded at the people in the planning office. He'd gone there to propose that they find among the Project Thanos volunteers a suicide who was physically and mentally capable of doing Carol's job. They said that they had tried, but there was no one suitable. He expressed his disbelief emphatically.)

Arnold Bates was in the primary chair in the control room. John Riley was in the backup.

"Take your position," Bates said. Carol lifted up the floater and held it over her head. She stood centered on the LMT crystal and the plastic cylinder slid down over her.

After a minute the cylinder rose again. "Get ready, Lefavre."

38
Second Contact

Carol landed on a high bluff over a river valley. She set down the floater and took a look around.

"There's a small city below me, at the junction of two rivers," she said. She had been instructed to give a verbal report. They hadn't said why but it was obvious: if she came back sliced up, as O'Brien had, they might not get the slice that had the camera tapes.

"Nineteen minutes. I can't make out much detail in the city, even under highest magnification. Moving specks that are vehicles. Oh—it's daytime. Achernar looks much smaller than the sun, but is painfully bright to look at, up to the last filter stop.

"I'll get on the floater, go down there and see if I can nab—wait." A round floater like the one that had approached O'Brien was settling out of the sky. "Here we go again."

It was a virtual replay of the first contact, except that the aliens on the floater were all female. Immediately after they landed, the long black ship followed, rushing in and then slowly settling on the grassy field, making the ground move under Carol's feet. The reflection of Achernar was a hard brilliant line down the ship's hull.

Again, the door dilated open, the ramp came down, and the aliens invited her aboard. There've been some changes made, though, Carol thought.

Among her vague instructions was the suggestion that she not turn on the magnetic field until she was actually threatened. She followed them up the ramp, turning to the right and left so that the cameras would get everything.

"So far, no aggressive moves," she said. They didn't stop at the entrance, the scene of the earlier slaughter, but led her on down the corridor.

They walked for a hundred meters so so. "A door opened on the right; they're taking me inside. . . . The walls are gray in this room. The ceiling and floor give off that yellow light. Sixteen minutes."

They led her to the far wall. "There's a real door here, a door that opens. Not just a seam. They want me to go through first. I'm motioning them through. After you, Alphonse."

The aliens won't understand, won't budge. "They must think I'm pretty stupid. Here goes."

She stepped toward the door but at the last moment grabbed one of the aliens by the shoulders and tossed her through first. She hit the floor with a hard bump, but did not get sliced to ribbons or explode or turn into a frog.

Carol stepped through and the woman scrambled away from her, staring expressionlessly. The door slammed shut and the room was dark. Carol turned on her suit lights.

"The walls and ceiling of this room are all metal except for a small window. The floor, too. Maybe they think it'll keep me from disappearing. Or from communicating. Think I'll wreck their door."

There was no latch on her side of the door, but the right-hand edge was a long ribbed strip like a piano hinge. She melted the hinge with four laser bursts and then pushed on the door.

As the door fell, the woman behind Carol jumped onto her back. She shrugged and flipped her across the room.

The door hit with a satisfying boom; curls of smoke rose from the hot edge as it melted a line on the floor. Three of the aliens edged back cautiously as she moved through the doorway.

Then the opposite wall opened and the fourth alien stepped through, cradling an armful of the microphone weapons. Carol plucked a grenade off her chest and threw it at the alien's feet.

The force of the blast staggered the woman, knocking her on her back. The weapons scattered.

The alien got back up. She had a thousand cuts from scalp to foot; the front of her body was a uniform red sheen. Her right foot was hanging on by a thin strip of flesh. When she put her weight on it the useless foot flopped aside and she walked on the shattered end of her exposed shinbone. She smiled at Carol with red pointed teeth and picked up a weapon. As she plugged it into her belt, Carol snapped the thumb switch that turned on her magnetic field.

And Carol sailed backwards into the metal room, slammed up against the wall, and stayed pinned there like an insect.

"Uh . . . the metal of this room is obviously magnetic. Thirteen minutes. Here they come."

She unclipped the yellow canister and tossed it in front of the aliens. The leader kicked it aside. She dropped the green one at her own feet.

Three of the aliens, including the mangled one, held back. The leader approached and said two syllables—then her eyes closed, her legs buckled and she fell to her hands and knees.

"Evidently the green tranquilizer works. . . . No." The alien shook her head and stood up again. "I'll hold off on the red for a few minutes." She smiled a shy, pretty smile: her teeth were white squares.

"I could have sworn all of them had pointed—" Carol flinched as the alien pointed the weapon at her. A hole opened in the hull a couple of meters away, letting in a beam of white light.

"It's working." The alien wiggled the weapon and the hole widened to a long gash. She nodded and walked back to the other three. She tried the weapon on the bloody one and it sliced her in two.

Carol closed her eyes and swallowed rapidly. They aren't human, she told herself over and over. They aren't even proper animals, they don't feel pain.

Deliberately looking away, she saw the alien who had first been in the room with her. It lay face-down on the floor, head against the wall.

"It looks like some of them are more vulnerable than others. One I threw against the wall is unconscious or dead."

She forced her eyes back to the others. "They're talking now, or growling. The . . . one they cut in two is also talking, lying on her back.

"That's strange. She doesn't look at all like the pictures we saw in training. Of slingshot accidents. It's . . . the body cavity doesn't have any identifiable organs. Just a lot of blood and yellow stuff. Here they come."

Three walked slowly toward her while the fourth, the truncated one, rolled up on one elbow to watch. Carol centered her, its, forehead in the crosshairs and tongued the laser. A black spot appeared there, smoldering, and the creature toppled over.

"They can be killed. It takes a head wound." The three others didn't even look back. "Ten minutes."

They tried all their wands on her simultaneously. She kept her arms flat against her sides; the beams glanced away and made latticework out of the thick hull. They grabbed her arms and shoulders and tried to pull her away from the wall.

"Maybe I can get you three." Their weapons were dangling free; she swept up the cords with one hand and jerked. The machines flew in a glittering arc across the room.

She hugged the three aliens to her, lacing her fingers behind them. They struggled, growling, bones grinding, but couldn't get free. "Nine minutes, I should be able to hold them. Unless re-inforcements come, with better weapons."

39

Chapter Eleven

Arnold Bates didn't look at the clock. "Thirty seconds."

"Lefavre!" Riley said. "Get out of that rifleman's line of sight. Get ready."

Rather get in the way of a dart than a laser, Jacque thought. He shuffled over and, with everybody else, focused all of his attention on the crystal.

"Fifteen seconds."

Carol and the three aliens materialized less than a meter above the crystal. She fell heavily but didn't topple, and held on to them. A piece of the ship's hull crashed beside her.

"Darts," Riley said.

"Two in each!" Carol shouted.

One of the aliens got three and sagged. The others relaxed and Carol loosened her grip on them.

"All right, Lefavre, bio team . . ." Suddenly all hell broke loose. The aliens squirmed out of Carol's grip and ran in different directions, toward the sandbags. "More darts," Riley shouted, but the order was unnecessary; the air was filled with the missiles, most of which missed and clattered harmlessly on the metal walls.

As they ran, the aliens changed shape.

Their torsos sprouted extra limbs—claws, tentacles, hairy spider arms. Beautiful faces grew monstrous with huge luminous eyes, terrible fangs. Seductive curves hidden by hair, scales, plates, feathers.

All different, all horrible, all bent on bloody murder.

One headed straight for the control room, leaping the last two meters, its shoulder toward the glass. "Kill them," Riley said as he grabbed Bates and both of them fell backwards to the floor.

The alien crashed into the glass just as the lasers started, lurid green pencils of energy crisscrossing in the air. The glass starred but didn't break. Two laser beams cut the alien into three unequal pieces, and shattered the glass.

It was over in seconds. The aliens had killed two people and injured seven, not counting the three who got serious burns. Jacque was unconscious with a concussion. Smell of burnt cloth and flesh and of hot metal and something else. The chamber was filled with gray haze from the smoldering sandbags.

Riley pulled himself up off the control room floor. The table was littered with blood-smeared glass. He surveyed the wreckage and adjusted his throat mike. "See if Lefavre's alive. Someone else pick up the bridge. . . . Maybe not all the creatures are dead yet."

"Look for one without a head wound." Carol said, her amplified voice booming into the stunned silence. "You can't kill them otherwise. Jacque?"

A medic was kneeling over Jacque, holding back his eyelids to check his pupils. "He'll be all right, I think," she said, and gave him an injection.

Riley was recovering. "Let's get an autopsy going here. . . . Physics, get a sample of that metal and run it down the hall. Is that one over in the corner alive?"

"Goddam right it is," someone said. "Tried to bite me." The alien had been sliced off just below the shoulders; it had one functioning tentacle and stubs of two other limbs. A laser had grazed its head—during the flurry of action Carol had shouted for them to aim there—taking off an ear and exposing a bluish brain mass. It lay on its back in a gory pool, tentacle twitching, growling in its throat.

"One of you suited Tamers grab the thing and restrain it. Who's got the bridge?"

"Lefavre's coming around," the medic said.

"Well, get him over there. How much time we have?"

Bates was back in his chair. "Seventeen minutes, fifty seconds. Then you have five minutes to get out. I have to steam and bake and dump the air. And stay away from my crystal. You've got it filthy already."

The loading crew came through a door carrying and pushing a new window and two ladders on rollers. They moved fast and stared straight ahead.

Carol got to the creature and grabbed its tentacle, pinning it under her arm. The alien tried to bite her on the wrist; she pulled its head back by the hair.

One of the Psych Group had the bridge. He approached rather timidly and touched it to the alien's chest.

"Not much," he said. "There's a sound, a word, that it repeats over and over. 'Liv . . . liver eye.'"

Jacque came over, stumbling, holding the side of his head. "Here, let me try." A creature had slugged him between the temple and eye; it was already swelling.

He bridged with the creature and instantly recoiled. "Jesus!" His face grew even paler. He hesitated and then made contact again.

"It . . . it's dying, I can tell that. I've never felt, never felt—there's so much hate here. Contempt. Disgust. . . . It sees me as a, as a soft . . . squishy thing, ugly. It would rather kill me than live, I think.

"There is one word. '*L'vrai*.' Maybe that's its name. Maybe the name of its race."

Jacque was silent for a minute. Then he set the bridge on the floor and sat back on his heels. "It's dead now." The creature continued to stare but had stopped growling.

"I made a kind of contact with the thing, just before it faded out. Nonverbal." He closed his eyes. "See if I can get it straight.

"If L'vrai is its name, it's also the name of the other two. It was checking, seeing whether the others were still alive. It's telepathic, at least in some limited way.

"I came closest to communicating when I allowed myself to

. . . hate it back. When I couldn't control my revulsion. It understood that.

"There's more. It's hard to put into words."

"That's all right," Riley said. "We'll see what we can get with hypnotics. Either of the other ones alive?"

Jacque was glad they weren't.

40
Autobiography 2053 (continued)

(From *Peacemaker: The Diaries of Jacque Lefavre*, copyright © St. Martin's TFX 2151:)

24 Jan 2053.

Spent most of today under hypnotics, the Psych group trampling around in my brain, trying to find out what that L'vrai said to me. They didn't seem too happy when they released me.

They have Carol now. She'll be home in an hour or so. We can sit and groan at each other. It's no fun to do it alone. They wouldn't give me anything stronger than APQ's—and an admonition not to drink any alcohol for eight hours, unless I wanted my stomach pumped. Couldn't be any worse than having your mind pumped.

I don't remember much of what I said to them; I was conscious and could hear myself talking, but the words didn't register. Guess I'll have to read the report.

Speaking of reports. Somebody put a clipping from Midnight TFX on the bulletin board outside the ready room; an exposé of the AED. Says there's no such thing as the Levant-Meyer Translation, men have never been to other planets, the holos and pictures are all faked (and Hollywood does a better job), the reams of official reports are all fiction. The AED is a hoax perpetrated by World Order members to maintain an expanding economy without allowing cash flow to nonmember enterprises in proportion to their contributions to the GWP. I suppose Midnight is owned by an Independent.

The article explains everything except this fucking bruise on my face. If those L'vrai were actors I hope they got paid well.

I was lucky, though. The same one who cuffed me killed two scientists by cracking their heads together.

Maybe I was also lucky that psychologist picked up the bridge and used it first on the L'vrai. It made the alien fourth in sensitivity, rather than third. And that was bad enough.

Still can't describe it. It was like seeing a color you've never seen before, a new primary color. The only thing familiar about the alien's thoughts was hate, and I've never felt any emotion so strongly with bridge. Not even from the Thanos people.

What will they do now? They got their autopsy and a little more behavioral information. And gave the L'vrai some information about us, I guess. Maybe they'll keep repeating the one-Tamer/minimum-time expedition until they stop learning new things.

Or they might take action. Gus told me there was some talk about attacking the aliens via the LMT. Pushing nuclear bombs through, dirty ones that would fill the planet's atmosphere with deadly isotopes.

Sounds stupid to me. What would we do if some aliens wiped out 61 Cygnus A? We'd have to go find them, and fight them, out of self-preservation.

And with the L'vrai we'd certainly lose the fight. They're technologically superior to us in most ways, as well as being shape-changers and natural telepaths. Naturally bloodthirsty, too. And when they go to a planet, they *stay* there, even if it takes them longer to get there.

It's enough to keep you awake nights. As Sweeney's report said, they might be in our backyard right now.

Carol's home.

41
All I Know Is What I Read in the Papers

SIRIUS WAVES
ALIEN THREAT?

PARIS, 13 JULY (WPI). Scientists here confirmed today that the gravity waves recently received from the vicinity of Sirius are of the same form and intensity as those which last October revealed the presence of L'vrai space ships near Achernar.

Sirius, less than nine light-years distant, is one of the closest stars to the Earth. It has a white dwarf companion and, so far as is known, no planetary system. It is too close to have been explored by the AED via the Levant-Meyer Translation.

The gravity waves were detected Monday by the Legrange satellites of Institut Fermi, at whose headquarters here an emergency conference met this morning.

An AED spokesman refused to comment on this new development, saying that an official statement is being prepared. . . .

AED FOES CLAIM
SIRIUS HOAX

LOS ANGELES, 14 July (IP). In a press conference here today the Union of Independent Scien-

tists charged that a conspiracy exists between Institut
Fermi and the Agency for Extraterrestrial Development.

They claim that the AED plans to capitalize on
public hysteria over the threat of a L'vrai invasion to
greatly increase their annual appropriation from the
World Order Council. This appropriation will come to
a vote next Wednesday, they point out; the coincidence is striking.

While admitting the existence of gravity waves
from Sirius, the UIS claims that Institut Fermi has
exaggerated the similarity between these and the
Achernar disturbance that last year led to the dis-
covery of the L'vrai.

They explained that the companion of Sirius is
an extremely dense white dwarf star. A minute change
in the angular momentum of the system could gen-
erate gravity waves similar to the ones detected by
Institut Fermi. . . .

AED ON SIRIUS HOAX:
NO COMMENT?

COLORADO SPRINGS, 14 July (WPI). An angry
spokesman for the AED at first refused to comment
today on the UIS charge that his organization had
deliberately misinterpreted data for the purpose of
increasing AED's appropriation next week.

John T. Riley, Director of AED Colorado Springs,
was reached at his home early this afternoon. When
queried on the UIS allegations, he said that they were
"beneath the attention of any intelligent person."

Riley at first refused to elaborate, but then gave
his opinion as a private citizen (noting that his views
did not necessarily agree with the official AED posi-

tion), accusing the UIS of "criminal cynicism," charging that the twenty-year-old union is "playing politics with the very survival of the human race."

Riley further claimed that the explanation of the Sirius gravity waves advanced by the UIS "could be disproved by a retarded undergraduate with a blunt pencil." He challenged the UIS to "come up with a mechanism, however absurd" that could change the total angular momentum of a stellar system without affecting the rotation and revolution rates of one of the stars. . . .

TRILLION-DOLLAR
AED BUDGET PASSES

STOCKHOLM, 23 July (IP). The World Order Council today passed by a narrow margin appropriations totaling $877,000,000,000 for the operation of the Agency for Extraterrestrial Development in fiscal 2053–4.

Opposition to the bill, which passed by a vote of 563 to 489, was headed by Minority Leader Jakob Tshombe (L., Xerox), who has threatened to resign his post in protest to the record-breaking budget.

Almost three times the size of last year's budget, most of the money is earmarked for the AED's Sirius crash program. The most expensive part of this program is the construction of a Levant-Meyer Translation facility on a planet circling Tau Ceti.

Critics of the program point out that the Sirius system is almost certainly planetless, and that the LMT requires a target planet. The AED, however, claims that at the range of Sirius from Tau Ceti (less than thirteen light-years), the target body need be no larger than a small asteroid. . . .

TAU CETI MISSION, 14 FEBRUARY 2054

PERSONNEL:
1. TAMER 7 TANIA JEEVES. FEMALE, 33. 11TH MISSION. SUPERVISOR.
2. TAMER 5 GUSTAV HASENFEL. MALE, 28. 8TH MISSION.
3. TAMER 4 (PROB) JACQUE LEFAVRE. MALE, 28. 7TH MISSION.
4. TAMER 3 CAROL WACHAL. FEMALE, 26. 4TH MISSION.
5. TAMER 2 VIVIAN HERRICK. FEMALE, 26. 3RD MISSION.

EQUIPMENT:
5 GPEM MODULES
1 PERSONNEL RECORDER
1 HOMING FLOATER (SECOND SHOT)
(ADDITIONAL EQUIPMENT WILL BE SUPPLIED ON TAU CETI FOR SECONDARY TRANSLATION TO SIRIUS SYSTEM (SEE ATTACHED SPECIFICATIONS))

POWER REQUIREMENT:
2 SHOTS 9.84699368131 SU, TUNING @ LOCAL TIME
07:45:28.28867BDK200561
07:48:11.38557BDK200560

MISSION PRIORITY 1.

FUNDING #999999 SIRIUS 90%
#000105 GEOFY 10%

Jacque and Carol went to Hell the week of its first rainfall.

Hell was the logical name for the only planet in Tau Ceti's biosphere. No bodies of standing water, constant dust storms, Sahara-like temperatures even at the polar regions.

They landed near the equator, where Tau was an amorphous white glare overhead, where abrasive clouds sped along the ground on hurricane winds almost hot enough to boil water. Dunes melted and formed with surreal swiftness around them and there was no horizon, only white sand at your feet and white sky overhead and a white storm all around.

The wind loved only flatness; it had long since ground every mountain and hill down for dust to fill the valleys, and it screamed displeasure at their height and tried to blow them down.

Jacque could tune out the shriek of the wind outside, but the suit's stabilizer moaned a wavering complaint as it fought to keep him upright. The sound all but deafened him, and made his teeth buzz.

Prudent animal instinct was telling him he'd be better off anyplace else. He resisted the urge to run blindly away, but did keep walking in nervous circles, looking for the floater. So did everyone else.

After a few minutes the floater appeared, tacking in against the wind. It bobbed like a bucking horse as they struggled on to it, then spiraled crazily up through the storm.

At about two thousand meters they hit a steady strong tailwind and started homing north, toward the polar settlement. Below them the top of the storm was an unbroken white surface, more like a snowscape than a maelstrom.

The storm began to break up as they moved north. Mottled ground was visible through twisting cyclone swirls of cloud. Eventually it turned hilly; nearing the pole they had to reach for altitude to clear the frost-dusted tops of mountains, Himalaya-sized but weathered into gentle lines.

And in a low bowl, protected by mountains on all sides,

a sudden alien splash of green. Gardenspot. They dipped over it but didn't land. The floater was homing toward where the LMT was being built, in another valley beyond.

It had taken six months to manufacture a crystal large enough to be practical and also free of internal flaws; a crystal with one microscopic bubble inside will explode with disconcerting force when you turn on the juice.

The crystal was in place and calibrated now, but the installation bore little resemblance to the streamlined efficiency of Colorado Springs. The first sign of it Tania's team saw was a glittering metallic spiderweb covering acres of mountainside —the antenna that collected power from an orbiting microwave laser. A few kilometers away the actual station sat, an aluminum dome dwarfed by four concentric rings of huge squat metal cylinders, which were the fuel cells fed by the antenna. Cables linked everything in a confusing but graceful skein of catenaries.

They landed on a small concrete square by the entrance to the dome, between two larger vehicles that were obviously of local design and manufacture. There was nothing green here, just dark red dust that crunched underfoot.

A man dressed only in shorts met them at the door. He led them around back to a crude winch arrangement, where they climbed out of their GPEM suits.

Inside, he gave them homespun shorts, and showed them the crystal.

"Ninety centimeters," he said. "I'm afraid it can only transport two at a time. Or one, with equipment."

"No facilities for sterilization," Tania said.

"Not really. We can seal off the dome and heat everything inside—specimens included, I'm afraid."

"It works, though?" Jacque said. "The crystal?"

"Sure. We've sent people to Sixty-one Cygnus and Vega."

"Not Sirius?"

"Not yet. We don't want to send anybody on a blind jump."

"You're still calibrating, then," Gus said.

"For Sirius, yeah. We've lost eight probes doing longer and longer jumps." The shorter a jump, the bigger its target has to be.

"That doesn't sound good," Tania said.

"Well, it means there's no planet in the system the size of earth or bigger . . . or maybe there is. Maybe the L'vrai destroy our probes before they can slingshot back.

"There's one due back tomorrow, a ten-day jump. You can spend the night in town and come back with me in the morning."

"Fine," Tania said. "It's been a long day."

He laughed. "Nothing *but* long days on this planet." Hell's axis was almost perpendicular to the ecliptic. Tau skimmed along the southern horizon for a ten-hour-long sunrise during the day; for night, they had ten hours of twilight.

They drove back to Gardenspot with the controller, whose name was Eliot Sampson. The ride on the electric truck was slow and bumpy.

They crawled up a long rise beyond which Sampson had said it was all downhill to town. When they got to the top, he slammed on the brakes.

"I'll be damned. Look at that." Suspended over Gardenspot was a large white-and-gray cloud. It was floating toward them.

"What," Jacque said, "A cloud?"

"Right, a cloud, a *cloud*." He put the truck in gear and lurched on down the hill. "I forgot," he shouted over the whining motor, "Today's the big cloud-seed experiment. See whether local rain can be . . . can compete with irrigation."

A few big drops spattered the windshield, leaving brown mud tracks in the dust. "Nothing but fossil water here," he said, "but lots of it. Underground lakes, rivers. We can pump it up, surround Gardenspot with standing water. Water vapor in the air." He laughed wildly.

Jacque had braced himself between the metal seat-back and the dashboard, knuckles turning white. "Say, aren't you going a little fast?"

"No, hell, all I ever do is drive this road. Want to get there before—" Suddenly they were drenched, blinded by a solid sheet of water. The rear wheels of the truck decided they wanted to lead for a while.

They spun around several times, wheels trying to find traction under the thin layer of sudden mud. Finally they slid into a ditch and came to a jarring halt. The first rain in a million years had caused the planet's first traffic accident.

The driver got a bloody nose and Jacque wrenched his shoulder, but there were no other injuries. The rain stopped while they were still pushing on the truck and listening to apologies.

"Sixty seconds now." Eliot Sampson looked up from the control board and, with the rest of the small crowd, stared at the waiting crystal.

"I just thought of something," Carol whispered.

"What's that?" Jacque said.

She took his hand. Her palm was moist and cold. "What if . . . what if the probe doesn't come back alone? What if some L'vrai is inside the slingshot radius?"

"Forty-five," Sampson said.

"Seems unlikely," Jacque said. "Crystal's not that big."

"Still. There isn't a weapon in this place."

Jacque shook his head. "Probe won't even come back, probably." He stepped to the wall and removed a heavy pair of bolt-cutters hanging there; he hefted the tool like a club. "Better than nothing."

Sampson looked at him quizzically. "Thirty seconds. What are you doing, Lefavre?"

Some of the others caught on. "Move up here, Jacque," Tania said. She was one of a half-dozen sitting closest to the crystal. "Just in case."

"Oh. I see," Sampson said. He started to count down from twenty. Jacque moved directly in front of the crystal and planted his feet in a wide solid stance. He had never played baseball or cricket, but he stared at the air over the crystal like a batter sizing up his strike zone.

"Zero—*God!*"

The probe was a squat black four-legged machine cluttered with instruments. Three severed tentacles clutched one side of it, pale white and writhing, spraying droplets of iridescent green fluid. Jacque half-swung and then stepped back.

The tentacles stopped squirming, relaxed, and dropped off. Tania broke the silence.

"I guess we do have a mission."

Later that day they looked at the tapes from the probe. It hadn't found a planet. It had come out of the LMT onto the hull of a L'vrai spaceship.

It sat on the long black hull undisturbed for days. Its holo camera revealed eight other L'vrai vessels, nearby, slowly orbiting Sirius. There might have been a thousand others, out of camera range.

Then a big spidery thing that could have been either a robot or an alien in a space suit—or just another L'vrai transmutation —scratched its way up the hull, captured the probe, and took it inside the ship through an iris in the hull.

It left the probe in an empty room, where it sat unmolested for hours. Then a L'vrai came in, shuffling awkwardly on four stiff legs: it had taken the form of the probe, perhaps to put the machine at its ease, perhaps for some less obvious motive.

The two machines regarded each other for some time. The probe's instruments recorded no sound, no electromagnetic signal that might have been an attempt at communication. They just looked at each other for ninety-three minutes; then the bogus probe waddled out.

It was replaced immediately by several L'vrai, in what was probably their natural form (if indeed they had a natural form). It was a versatile shape, rather like an octopus with a flexible skeleton. They had six or eight—varying with the individual—

large tentacles that could serve as feet or crude two-fingered hands. A tubular thorax broadened into a scalloped crest at the top, where it sported three eyes; one large fixed one and two smaller eyes on articulated stalks, which waved from the corners of the crest. Under the fixed eye was a slit that occasionally curled open to reveal parallel rows of black shark-like teeth set in foamy mucus.

Several small tentacles sprouted from under the crest, ending in various arrangements of fingers, hooks, and suckers. Some of them changed form as they watched.

Most of the body was a waxy, off-white color (the eyes were amber); the thorax was transluscent, revealing dark pulsing shadows of organs. In the back were two slits that might have been excretory, genitals, or watch pockets.

They were too odd-looking to be disgusting or terrifying.

One of the L'vrai came in pushing a cart that hovered wheelless over the floor. It had two tiers of shiny metal instruments. He squatted down by the probe and the others watched as he fiddled with the machine.

Most of what he did was out of the camera's range. But after a few minutes of what looked like a parody of "scalpel . . . sponge . . . retractors . . ." he managed to disconnect or short out the power source, and the picture went dark.

Sampson spun the tape ahead; there was nothing more on it.

"That's it," he said. "What would you like to see again?"

"Run it back to where they took the probe off the outside of the ship," Tania said. "We'll look at the whole thing again. And again. And get everybody who's not on some vital duty to come study it.

"Jacque, Carol, you better go get some sleep. Get pills; sleep for a couple of days if you can."

Carol nodded. "Ten-day jump?"

"We can't take a chance on a shorter one, not on such a small target. So it'll probably be ten days without sleep."

"What about you?"

"I'll be along. I want to go through the tape once more and then set up the jump parameters with Eliot." She patted Carol on the shoulder. "I don't need as much sleep as you youngsters."

"Youngsters," Jacque said. "See you later, Mom. Don't stay up too late."

They went by the medical building to get sleeping pills and tell the woman in charge how they needed to modify the pharmaceutical systems in their GPEM suits. She said she could set up the personnel recorder to monitor the level of fatigue poisons in their blood, and compensate with small doses of joy juice. It would be a strain, though. They'd pay a big price when they got back—narcolepsy alternating with paranoic insomnia. And old-fashioned cold turkey.

That's all right, they said. Cross that bridge, etc.

They went to the transients' longhouse, pushed two of the narrow, hard beds together, and unfolded privacy screens around them.

Undressed, Jacque stretched out on the bed and stared at the ceiling. Carol nestled up next to him. He scratched her back listlessly.

"Ten days," Jacque said. "We aren't going to make it."

"Don't talk that way."

"God knows what those monsters can come up with in ten days."

"It doesn't do any good to worry about it."

"Riley didn't say anything about ten days."

"He couldn't have known. We had a chance to say no."

"Sure. But it gets to me. I don't feel like dying this particular—"

"Stop it!"

"Sorry. Thinking aloud. We have the magnets, we might be all right."

"We will," she whispered. She rolled over and pulled him to her and held him fiercely. "We will."

43
Job Description

It is 22 January 2054 and John Riley enters the conference room and says hello to the five people seated around the seminar table. He passes each one of them a single sheet of paper:

Mission Chronology:

PHASE I:
24 Jan. Passive courier to Groombridge 1618. He will remain on Groombridge for 21 days, obtaining two bridges, detoxified by Thanos volunteer. Without touching the bridges himself, he will bring them back to Tamers Lefavre and Herrick.

PHASE II:
14 Feb. Tamer Jeeves's team to Tau Ceti, 21 days.

PHASE III-A:
Date and duration to be set by Jeeves, Tau Ceti controller. LMT from Tau Ceti to Sirius: Jeeves, Lefavre (with bridge), and Wachal. Priorities: Gather information, survive, attempt to communicate, engage L'vrai in combat. Return with artifacts or prisoner if possible.

PHASE III-B:
Date and duration to be set by Hasenfel, Tau Ceti controller. If Jeeves, Lefavre, and Wachal do not return, Hasenfel and Herrick attempt the same mission (Herrick with bridge).

PHASE IV:
17 Feb. Research team to Tau Ceti, 12 days.

PHASE V: Repeat Phase III as often as practical.

PHASE VI:
7 Mar. Slingshot translation to Earth.

Tania scratches her head. "Doesn't tell us much, really."

"I know," says Riley. "All we can say for sure is that the Tau Ceti crystal is working. We got a note yesterday on a slingshot from a Sixty-one Cygni resupply mission, said they'd gotten a probe from Tau Ceti. We want to get you there as soon as possible."

"May I ask . . . why us?"

"Well, the logic is clear. I know you aren't the most experienced team available, not by a wide margin. But you do have Wachal," he nods at her, "who has encountered the L'vrai on their own territory before, and Lefavre," again, "who is more sensitive to the Groombridge Effect than any other Tamer. And besides, he's bridged with the L'vrai before."

"That's true," Jacque says, "but my experience there would indicate you want somebody who's *not* sensitive to the Effect. Not the other way around. They're powerful."

"This has been taken into account," Riley says. "This is why Tamer Herrick is holding the second bridge. She is relatively insensitive to the Effect, and Tamer Hasenfel is even less sensitive. If necessary, the bridge can be exposed to multiple contacts among the Tau Ceti personnel before Hasenfel touches it. So we are capable of a wide spectrum of sensitivity."

"In case it burns out my brain on the first try," Jacque says flatly.

"I wouldn't put it so extremely. We admit the possibility—even a high probability—of psychological damage. But the Psych Group assures me that such damage would be reversable. And therapy would begin immediately; Dr. Sweeney himself will be on the Phase IV research team."

"Therapy as part of debriefing," Jacque says.

Riley exhales through his nose, twice, and says, "I can understand your apprehension, Lefavre. But one is a Tamer or one is not. You may refuse any mission."

"In a sense."

"In an absolute sense. All you have to do is say no."

Jacque chuckles lightly. "And miss seeing Sirius? Not on your life, Mr. Riley. No sir, not for the world."

"That's the spirit, Lefavre." Riley looks around the table. "Now that goes for everyone. I don't deny that this is a perilous mission. If you want out, now's the time. No trouble to make replacements at this stage."

Nobody says anything. Riley stands up. "Well, I've got to move on. Tomorrow you'll go down to the Krupp factory and be fitted with modified GPEM's, magnetic ones like Tamer Wachal used on Achernar. . . . Thank you. You're a good team."

The door sighs shut behind him. After a respectful interval of silence, Tamer Jacque Lefavre delivers his opinion:

"Shit. Oh, shit."

44

Chapter Thirteen

Tania went first. A ten-day jump to Sirius took enough power to almost completely drain the crystal's fuel cells. Jacque and Carol had to wait forty-five minutes while they recharged.

"Wonder if we'll find one another," Jacque said, standing by the crystal watching Sampson watch a dial.

"That's up to Tania." She had the floater.

"You can take your positions now," Sampson said. "About two minutes." Vivian and Gus raised their hands in a good-luck gesture. They were the only spectators—standing by GPEM-suited, in case something went wrong.

After two minutes the control room suddenly disappeared and Jacque floundered in total darkness. "Carol!"

She had been standing on his shoulders. "I'm here, Jacque . . . floating somewhere."

His retinas were adjusting to the darkness. A few stars were visible. Sheepishly he remembered he'd set his optical circuits for the bright control room. He twisted the knob that controlled the sensitivity all the way to the left: stars grew bright all around him and, under his feet, the shiny black hull of a L'vrai ship.

Carol's helmet appeared above his head; then her shoulders. She was moving out of the spaceship's shadow, into the light from Sirius.

"I see you now. Are your boots on?" Their boots had magnetic soles.

"Yes, but I guess I'm too far away. Turn on your lights, give me something to aim at."

Jacque did and Carol rotated slowly around, then threw him a line and he hauled her in.

"Go see what the other side looks like?" Jacque said.

"Just a second." She wound the slender cable into a tight coil and slid it back into her thigh pocket. "Get anything from Tania?"

"No, not yet."

"That's not good." Tania could be as much as a million kilometers away, much too far to travel on the floater in ten days. Or she might be on the other side of the ship.

They walked around to the other side. Sirius was a bright dot the size of a pinhead; its dwarf companion, a faint point almost lost in the glare.

"Jacque?" Tania's voice was soft and blurred with static. "Carol? Do you read me?"

They both answered at once. "Wait," Tania said. "Give me a time reading; see how far away you are."

Jacque watched the digits shining just above his faceplate display. "Coming up on 11:14 . . . mark."

"Damn," she said. "Second and a half, that's a good half-million kilometers. Looks like we work alone."

"Guess so," Jacque said. "Where are you," Carol said, "are you on a ship?"

Three-second lag. "No, you're on a ship?"

"On the outside of one, yeah," Jacque said. "You found a planet, an asteroid?"

"A rock, anyhow. Maybe two kilometers long."

"Will you just stay there," Carol asked, "or go off looking for trouble?"

"I've been looking for ships. Don't want to take off without a—wait. Think I see one. Like a dim star but elongated. A short little line of light."

"That would be starlight reflected off the—"

"It wasn't there before, I'm sure of it. They're coming after me. . . . Yes, it's getting closer."

Jacque felt a vibration in his boots just as Carol said "Behind you!"

A man-sized black spidery machine, like the first artifact

the probe had encountered, came clicking across the hull toward him. "Get around to the other side," Jacque said. "Then turn on your magnet. I'll do the same here."

Tania's voice whispered, "Trouble?"

"We'll see." The machine didn't appear to have any weapons. It approached Jacque and extended a pincered arm. He took one step forward, turned on his magnet . . .

And slammed chest-first to the hull, pinning the machine underneath him. It squirmed like a live thing, then emitted a shower of sparks—Jacque's short hair tingled with the static electricity—and lay still.

"It's a machine," Jacque said; "I crushed it. Are you standing upright?"

No answer. "Carol! Are you standing upright?"

"Jacque," Tania said, "if she's on the other side of the ship, she can't hear you. Line-of-sight transmission."

Jacque felt his face warm. "That's right. Say, how are you doing, is it still coming closer?"

"Yes. Not very fast. I think I'll play with it a little bit. See how maneuverable it is."

Jacque turned off his magnet. "I'm going to go check on Carol. Good luck."

"Same to you." He stood up and was surrounded by a cloud of floating metal fragments. Most of the machine lay flattened out, stuck to the hull by weak residual magnetism.

In the center of the wreck a bluish mass had oozed out and dried in the vacuum: the remnants of a L'vrai brain.

He walked around to where Carol was standing. From the crash of static in his ears, he knew that her suit was magnetized.

"What happened?" she shouted.

"Fell on top of it and crushed it. It's a machine with a L'vrai brain attached."

"Have to be careful walking."

"Forgot. Turned it on with one foot in the air."

"Vacuum," she corrected. "We better do the back-to-back. There'll be more."

"Okay." He backed up against her and thumbed the switch that magnetized his suit. They *clicked* together; the suits had been set up with opposite polarity so they could operate this way.

Nothing happened. After a half hour: "Carol, they aren't going to come to us while we're magnetized. Not after what happened to the last one."

"I guess not."

"Want to switch them off and go exploring?"

"No, wait. They must know where we are. They might be waiting right under our feet. Zap us as soon as we turn off the field."

"Wait like this for ten days?" Actually, the prospect wasn't unappealing to Jacque. At least they were relatively invulnerable.

"No. I have an idea. . . . Stay right where you are." Carol turned off her field and knelt down, apparently studying the hull under their feet.

"What are you—oh." Her laser glared. Where it punched through the hull, a long plume of air drifted out. She continued cutting in an arc, centered around Jacque's feet. Air had stopped leaking out before she was halfway around.

"Now," she said, a few centimeters from completing the circle—

And they were falling in darkness.

They landed on something hard; Jacque stood up and turned on his lights.

"Artificial gravity." They were standing in a wedge-shaped room, the floor a section of a circle. In one corner was a large round pillow; the only other piece of furniture was something that looked like a filing cabinet, but without handles.

A mass of tentacles protruded from the far wall, the side closest to the space ship's central axis. They walked cautiously over to investigate.

"It's the bottom part of a L'vrai," Carol said.

"Yeah. Got stuck trying to get out of the room, looks like." Jacque prodded the wall. It was slightly resilient. "Don't see any seam. When you went through these things before . . . could you tell where they were before they opened?"

"No, but I didn't really have time to—"

"Here!" Jacque's finger disappeared into the wall. He pulled it out, pushed it back in, moved it up and down. "You can't see it, no, but this is where it is." He got both hands into the seam and tried to pull it open. It wouldn't give.

"You take one side here; I'll take the other." Enough force to tie a knot in a steel girder, but nothing happened. Jacque put his arm in up to the elbow, and quickly withdrew it.

"What do you think?" Jacque said. "I guess we could just walk through it."

"Let me take a look first." Carol put her head against the wall and pushed; her helmet disappeared up to the shoulders.

She tilted forward and disappeared.

Jacque leaped after her; slammed against the wall. He pushed hard. Nothing happened. Calming, he pressed his hand across the wall until he found the seam, then leaned into it.

Vertigo: a well-lit elevator shaft 50 stories high. Jacque staggered back.

Bracing himself against the "doors," he peered through again. Carol was floating on the other side of the shaft. "Come on in," she said. "No gravity here." With one hand she held on to a metal rod that ran the length of the shaft, like a fireman's pole.

Jacque eased through the slit, stepping over the inert L'vrai body. The entrance acted like a flexible gasket, sealing itself around his suit as he passed through, keeping the vacuum out.

He treaded air and drifted toward the metal pole, the suit's magnetism pulling him. Carol moved her hand just in time to keep from getting pinned between him and the pole.

"What now?" he said. "Up or down?"

"Up's closer." The shaft ended some twenty meters over

their heads. "I'm going to switch on again. . . . This place frightens me."

"Yeah. Any moment I expect an army of them to come pouring out of the wall." They worked their way up the pole hand-over-hand. The grip they had to exert to overcome the force of their magnetic fields was so great that their fingers left indentations in the metal.

Almost to the top, Carol said "Try infrared." Jacque did; the entrance slits suddenly were visible, slightly lighter than the surrounding wall.

"Well, now we have someplace to go. Question is—"

"Do we go there, or let them come to us?" Carol said. "I vote we stay here for a while."

"I don't know," Jacque said. "Maybe we ought to keep the initiative."

"And maybe they've set a trap. They've had time."

Jacque thought for a moment. "Maybe we ought to burn our way through one. We should be able to do it at this distance, not get too close to them."

"All right. You choose."

Jacque aimed at the seam directly in front of him. With one short burst, it opened along its whole length and sagged—

And the spear of energy continued through the room beyond, to an assembly of heavy machinery arranged along the opposite wall. Some delicate balance was disturbed; some false signal initiated:

The wall was a loading bay. It snapped open to empty space.

Jacque and Carol were buffeted by the hurricane force of air being sucked out of the ship. All up and down the corridor, seams dilated open. Several L'vrai slid into the shaft, writhing in death throes. One passed by them to tumble on into space. Then the wind died, for lack of air.

After a long while, Jacque said "Makes sense. . . ."

"What?"

"The seams. They're only rigid against vacuum from one

direction. No natural disaster's going to fill the corridor with vacuum without breaching the outer shell."

"We're an unnatural disaster, then?"

They watched an alien float by, inert and cooling.

For ten days they divided their time between scouting the wreckage and anxiously keeping a lookout for other L'vrai ships. It seemed unlikely that the ⌐est of the flotilla would be ignorant of the disaster that had befallen one of their number.

But ignoring it, Jacque argued, was consistent with the way they acted toward one another. Even toward themselves.

Jacque or Carol often ventured outside of the ship, trying to contact Tania. They never had any success.

When slingshot time approached, they gathered a selection of small artifacts and assumed the feet-on-shoulders position.

"Rape," Jacque said. "Then pillage. *Then* burn."

"What?"

"Never mind. Old joke."

45
Messenger

When Jacque and Carol appeared, there were a lot of people gathered under the dome that housed the crystal. Only one was looking at them, the controller.

"Are you hurt?" Sampson said. "Are you all right?"

Jacque tongued his outside channel and answered in chorus with Carol that they were all right. "What's going on?"

"Jeeves came back . . . catatonic. You're all right, though?"

"Hell, yes. Get us out of these damned tanks!" To Carol: "That's why we couldn't get through to her . . . must have been within a couple of hours—"

"—when she saw the ship," Carol said. "What could it have been?"

Something I'm glad I didn't see, Jacque thought. She's a tough old bird.

Sampson led them around back and helped them out of their suits. "Doc says bring along the bridge," he told Jacque. "Maybe you can get through to her."

She was lying on a cot in a room next to the crystal, surrounded at a distance by a large circle of people. A fold of cloth covered a token of her nakedness. She was pale and flaccid and seemed not to be breathing; only her eyes showed life. They moved behind bruised slits.

When Jacque and Carol broke through the circle, Tania tried to sit up. The doctor pushed her back down with his knuckles, trying not to poke her with the empty hypodermic needle he held.

"Lie still for a moment. I'm trying to find a vein." He kneaded the inside of her elbow with his thumb. "Blood test," he said in Jacque's direction. He made a pinch of skin and slid the needle in.

The transparent cylinder filled up with yellow fluid.

The doctor dropped the hypodermic as if stung. "L'vrai!"

It stood up and swept him aside with a casual backhand to the chest. It pointed at Jacque.

They all shrank back. "I'll get the laser," somebody said. They had one mounted by the crystal, in case.

"Can't," Sampson said. "It's permanently mounted."

Jacque was standing his ground, staring at the thing that looked like Tania. "Get me a wrench, anything. I'll kill it."

The L'vrai shook its head, growled, and stepped toward Jacque.

A heavy ball-peen hammer slid across the floor to Jacque's feet. He dropped the bridge and picked it up.

The Tania-image shimmered, flowed, grew. It became a handsome man, tall with gray hair: Robert Lefavre at his prime.

"Good trick," Jacque said, hefting the weapon. "Won't work, though."

The creature took two impossibly large steps and was in front of Jacque. He swung at the head but it dodged, and the hammer crunched through collarbone; flesh grew up and over the metal. Jacque pulled on it but it was fast.

The creature seized Jacque by the arm and forced him to the ground. It picked up the bridge and pressed it against his chest.

Jacque's face contorted with terror. "I—

"I—

"I can . . ." He suddenly calmed. "I can speak to you through this one. We have certain things in common."

46
Autobiography 2034

986. I will never hurt cats or dogs again.

987. I will never hurt cats or dogs again.

988. I will never hurt cats or dogs again.

989. I will never hurt cats or dogs again.

990. I will never hurt cats or dogs again.

991. I will never hurt cats or dogs again.

992. I will never hurt cats or dogs again.

993. I will never hurt cats or dogs again.

994. I will never hurt cats or dogs again.

995. I will never hurt cats or dogs again.

996. I will never hurt cats or dogs again.

997. I will never hurt cats or dogs again.

998. I will never hurt cats or dogs again.

999. I will never hurt cats or dogs again.

1000. I will never hurt cats or dogs again.

—Jacque Lefavre

47

Chapter Fourteen

Most of the crowd stood frozen, staring. Sampson was edging toward the door.

"None of you will attempt to leave, or to harm me. Normally that would be of little consequence. But it would be awkward, here and now.

"I could kill any or all of you without touching you. I would demonstrate on one but from what I understand of your nature, you would not take the logical course. This is my problem in dealing with you: you evolved a kind of intelligence, but too quickly. Your animal nature was kept separate, not properly assimilated.

"Who is in charge here?"

A black, gray-haired woman stepped forward. "I am Sara Bahadur. Coordinator of Research, Sirius Project."

"But you cannot speak for all humans."

She smiled. "No one can do that."

"But there are those who can speak for larger numbers."

"Yes."

"Bring them to me. Now."

"That isn't possible. They're all on earth."

"This isn't earth, then. Your home planet."

"No. It's very far away."

"But you can travel between here and earth instantaneously. In a sense."

"That's true."

"I repeat: bring them to me."

"And I repeat, that isn't possible. Not in ten . . ."

"How long?" She didn't answer. "Don't worry about giving away secrets. I, the I-that-was-then, knew about this transportation process when—" He paused, evidently searching Jacque's mind. "—you humans were still in trees. I abandoned it as too limiting. How long?"

"Ten days. A day is—"

"I know."

"I could take you to them."

"No. I will not be in the presence of many humans. I perceive directly your . . . your subconscious beings. It would be distressing. I could not function. It is difficult enough here.

"Go to your planet and bring back such leaders as will come. Have this one well so that I can talk through him. I will go away until they come."

"Wait," Bahadur said. "You want to meet with all the leaders of humanity, but you haven't established who you are. A spaceship pilot? What gives you authority to speak for all L'vrai?"

"The question is meaningless. I go now."

"But how will we find you? Where are you go—"

"You will not find me. I will know when to come back. From this mind I see that we are surrounded by desert and mountain. That is where I will be."

"Do you need food and water?" someone said.

"Only solitude." It released Jacque and the bridge and stood up. The figure of Jacque's father dissolved, then rose again as a python-sized serpent, covered with shimmering golden scales. It slithered to the door and out.

Carol broke the silence. "Jacque!" He was lying limp, his eyes rolled back, saliva drooling out of the corner of his mouth. She ran and kneeled by him and cradled his head between her breasts. She rocked back and forth with her eyes squeezed shut, making tight noises in her throat.

It took a minute for the doctor to pry her gently away.

48
Psychiatrist's Report

It is 14 April 2035. Drs. Mary and Robert Lefavre sit in a well-appointed psychiatrist's office in New York City. He is Dr. Chaim Weinberg, a child psychiatrist who specializes in the problems of gifted children.

Weinberg opens the slim folder on his desk. "Well, there's no question that Jacque is a brilliant child." He traces his finger along the top sheet. "His IQ is 188 on the Modified Stanford-Binet (181 on the acultural version); his reading ability is that of the average college junior. Thematic Apperception and vocational preference tests . . . reveal a creative and challenge-seeking personality. He has as great a potential for success and happiness as I've ever seen in a child." He looks at them expectantly.

Robert supplies his punctuation: "But."

"Well, as you know, he doesn't get along with the other children."

"That's putting it mildly," Mary says.

"Dr. Lefavre, if I didn't put things mildly to parents, I'd run out of patients in short order." They share an urbane chuckle at Dr. Weinberg's situation.

"I've had two talks with Jacques now, with Jacques under hypnosis. He believes that all of his classmates are either close allies or bitter enemies. No one in between."

"Is that so unusual?" Robert says. "I think I felt the same way at his age."

"Only unusual in its intensity and absoluteness. Most children are at least mildly paranoid. In your boy's case, though, he sees the situation exactly backward. I've interviewed his teachers and social worker: they say he has a few close friends, but all of the other children are afraid of him. His unpredictable outbursts of violent temper—"

"They gang up on him!" Robert says sharply.

"Well, he's a head taller than any of them, and stronger."

"You aren't suggesting we move him up another year?" Mary says.

"No. The others are already a year or two ahead of him in . . . the puberty sweepstakes. But as I say, the others don't really hate him. In an odd way, they respect him. He'll help anyone with his homework, without being arrogant about it, and he doesn't show off his intelligence in the classroom. You trained him in that."

"I was in his shoes once," Robert says.

"Yes, of course. But the net result of this is . . . well, in playground jargon, they say he has a diode loose. That affair with the animals last year didn't help."

"That was blown all out of proportion," Robert says evenly. "Scientific curiosity. He thought he had anesthetized them."

Weinberg squares the stack of paper in front of him and stares at it. Softly: "That's not what he says under hypnosis."

49
Chapter Fifteen

Jacque was dreaming that they had inserted a long needle into his brain. They screwed a syringe onto it and sucked out yellow fluid.

"Darling! Jacque! Wake up." Carol was shaking him hard.

Jacque shook his head and patted her on the shoulder. "Nightmare." The sheet was twisted around him, soaked. He worried at it but only made the situation worse; swore, and jerked, tearing the fabric.

"Here, let me." Carol got off the cot and unwound him, from the feet up. "Poor helpless creature." She slid into bed next to him. Held him.

"Look, if you want to do that, let's switch sides. This one's all clammy."

"Okay." She rolled over onto her cot and Jacque followed. "Are we alone?" he asked.

"Far as I know. Nobody's come in since I woke up." He started caressing her. "Look, that, that's not necessary. I've been waiting for you for an hour."

He laughed softly and eased himself onto her.

"We can go an easier way," she said. "Long day ahead of you."

He answered with a first slow thrust. "Call this work?"

The door to the billet slammed open. Sampson's voice came through the privacy screen: "You up, Lefavre?"

"In a manner of speaking." Carol giggled into his chest.

"Well, the last bunch of VIP's came in. They're about two hundred klicks away and homing."

"All right. Give me five minutes."

"Ten!" Carol said: "Jackrabbit," she whispered.

"I'll be outside in the truck."

* * *

It wasn't much of a conference room: a dissection table covered with homespun, surrounded by folding chairs and stools. Nobody sat. Pacing around the room were six of the most important people in the world:

Hilda Svenbjørg, pale, thin, chain-smoking; a touch of blonde in her ruff of white hair. World Order Council Majority Leader (C., Westinghouse).

Jakob Tshombe, light chocolate skin, expressionless features more Caucasian than Negroid, standing patiently. World Order Council Minority Leader (L., Xerox).

Pacing were Bill ("Hawkeye") Simmons, leader of the Union of Independent Scientists; Reza Mossadegh, Coordinator of the World Petroleum Cartel; Fyodor Lomakin, Premier of the Eastern Grain Bloc; and Chris Silverman, leader of the World Council of Churches and Western Pope (her eyebrows shaved California-style).

They were ignoring Jacque and the other three Tamers. Carol and Vivian and Gus were in their GPEM suits, acting as bodyguards. Jacque sat on a stool in the middle of the room, next to a bowl of water that held the bridge.

A hissing sound from outside: the last arrivals. Jacque and Bahadur went out to greet them.

Tethered to the floater were three man-sized cannisters, like overgrown oil drums: static life-support units. You can't put an untrained person (or a pregnant woman, past a couple of months) into a GPEM suit; these LSU's could keep a person alive, if immobile, for several weeks in any environment.

With the help of the floater pilot, they unscrewed the tops of the cannisters; three undignified dignitaries came out. They limped into the conference room and Bahadur addressed all nine.

"I don't know how much time we have, so I'll give a brief summation of what we know. Which isn't much. Then answer questions.

"You know that the L'vrai are an ancient race, and that they can assume virtually any shape, evidently by an exercise of will—"

"I'll believe that when I see it," Hawkeye Simmons muttered.

"You will see it, I believe.

"They appear to be telepathic with one another. Since the Sirius L'vrai are in possession of information that L'vrai on Achernar and Earth learned only months ago, then their telepathic messages must travel at greater speeds than that of light. Perhaps instantaneously."

"Impossible by information theory," Simmons said.

"How interesting. Their telepathy works only imperfectly with human beings; evidently they can read our minds only at some preconscious level."

"Can you be sure of this?" Tshombe asked. "We will be at a considerable disadvantage in negotiating if our thoughts are open to him."

"There is objective evidence of a sort. When the L'vrai first appeared in human form, they . . . their sexual parts were exaggerated in a way that suggested the totems of primitive peoples. And they were unblemished, handsome idealizations of the self-images of the people with whom they were in contact.

"I myself saw this L'vrai take the form of his communicant's—" nodding at Jacque—"father. Evidently to inspire trust. It was the image of his father when the Tamer was a small, vulnerable boy.

"The L'vrai, the one who spoke with us, only used the first person singular pronoun—even when referring to his entire race. This means either that the race literally has only one consciousness—"

"Patently—"

"—or that his syntax reflects a philosophy that subordinates the individual's worth to the idea of his membership in some larger group, or his relationship to a spiritually higher—"

A golden snake slithered through the open door.

The blood drained from Simmons's face.

Silverman crossed herself.

Mossadegh clutched his throat.

Svenbjørg put out her cigarette and Tshombe raised one eyebrow.

The serpent's head weaved at their level for a few moments. Then it continued drifting toward Jacque. Its scales hissed on the rough concrete.

Musky smell of nervous sweat.

"Is it . . ." Silverman began.

"Is it what?" Bahadur said.

"Is it going to hurt him?"

"Not physically. I don't think. If it does we know how to kill it."

The L'vrai raised itself as if to strike, towering over Jacque. Jacque bared his teeth and started to rise.

Then the snake blurred and melted and reformed as a bent old man clad in a white toga. His face was full of benevolent wrinkles and he had only a few strands of white hair. He could have been any race: his skin was the color of age and his features the shape of a saint's.

The illusion would have been perfect except that the toga showed a barely perceptible network of yellow veins.

It reached into the bowl and took out the bridge, then offered it to Jacque. Jacque touched it and snapped to his feet, galvanized, face and body rigid with pain. Then he slumped back onto the stool and began to speak.

"You are curious about me. Ask anything."

Tshombe's voice was flat and authoritative: "Why are you here? What do you want with us?"

"That depends on what you mean by 'here.' I am in this region of space because I am expanding my sphere of influence, as you are. I am in this room for your convenience. To explain your situation."

"And what do you mean by 'I'?" Svenbjørg said. "Is there only one of you, or many?"

"In your sense there are many, there are billions. But really there is only one. Only L'vrai."

"Which brings us back to where we started," Bahadur said. "Do you mean this in a literal sense? If we killed half your billions you would not be diminished?"

"Only in the potential for exploring and manipulating the volume of space that surrounds me. If only one of me was left it would still be completely me, L'vrai.

"This could be true of humans as well. In a sense, it is true. You blind yourselves to it."

"Theology," Hawkeye Simmons muttered.

"No," the L'vrai said, "it's a simple fact. I am many but I am one. All identical."

"What you mean is that you're clones. All stamped out of the same mold."

Jacque was silent while the creature searched his brain for the term. "In no sense. I am only one and have always been only one. Only L'vrai."

"Each of your parts is aware of every other one?" Svenbjørg asked. "They act with common purpose?"

"You are asking the same question over and over. The answer, again, is 'yes.' Please ask something—"

"He could well be lying," Mossadegh said.

"There would be no reason for it. I have absolute power over you. The ones in this room and the billions on Earth as well. And on the other planets, if they were worth destroying."

"I don't believe you," Tshombe said. "From this room you can—"

"Did you listen to me? I am not only in this room."

"Even so—"

"I will explain in detail, then. Yes, I could kill all or most of you in this room by creating what this one calls a 'feedback' condition in your brains. This body of mine would also die.

"Killing your other billions will take longer. That's what the ships at the near blue star . . . Sirius, are for. With a relatively simple maneuver they can upset the harmony of forces inside your sun, and make it explode."

"Why?" Silverman broke the silence, her voice quavering. "Why in the holy name of God would you want to do that?"

"Is that a serious question?" No one replied. "It seems so obvious. You are expanding through my volume of space. I must either destroy you or arrive at a compromise as to . . . the use of this region."

"That's why you're here, then?" Simmons said. "To negotiate over who gets what?"

"You do not listen either. As I said, I am here to explain your situation. There will be no negotiating." It paused. "Would you negotiate with an ant over the rights to a piece of sugar? The rights to your house?"

"You called this meeting to gloat, then?" Simmons was almost shouting. "Why not just sneak up and blow us to hell without any warning?"

The L'vrai smiled. "That might have been the most humane course."

"Humane," Silverman scoffed. "You *enjoy* killing people. Don't deny it, I've seen the cubes. You just want to prolong—"

Jacque made a noise between a laugh and a death rattle. "You poor . . . ignorant creatures. I should explain—have explained.

"I did enjoy, yes, killing those people. Insofar as it was my duty to them." He waited for them to quiet down. "Exactly that, my duty.

"I am an ethical and . . . the closest you say is 'courteous' . . . organism. My first act when I meet a new organism is to do what it expects me to do. As well as I can divine its wishes."

"I can not believe this," said Chin (L., Bellcomm). "These people, you claim, wanted you to kill them?"

"Not precisely. They expected me to *try*. Physically. Simply to kill them, with no danger to my own parts, would have been easy enough."

"I believe him." It was Gustav Hasenfel, the first Tamer to speak. His amplified voice rang off the metal walls. "We're always ready for trouble; always expect the worst."

"Thank you," it said. "This one understands, too." The wise old face looked down at Jacque with something like affection. "But he knew from the first time he touched my mind, on earth. Though he didn't know how to say it.

"This one is different from most of you. He has brought the animal part of his nature into harmony with the . . . angel part. He does not attempt to separate them. Because of this, he and I can talk. I can sense that no one else in this room possesses this kind of, this kind of integration. You keep your animals and angels separate: you would have the angel prevail. It never can.

"For this reason, we can't waste time. This one dies, and without him I can no longer speak."

The table of people was between Carol and the L'vrai. She shuffled sideways to take aim.

"*Tamer!*" Bahadur shouted. "*Don't*"—drowned out by Hasenfel's booming voice: "*Look away I'll kill you first.*"

Carol's helmet swiveled toward her teammate, crystal clusters of optical sensors below the terrible red eye. "You would," she said.

"And then myself," he said. "I'm sorry, Carol."

"Then have the L'vrai do it." She turned up her vocals and her cracked whisper filled the room. "Do you hear me, monster?"

"I will kill you if you turn your weapon on me." Jacque's strained voice said. "Not otherwise. Now that I know how you believe you can individually die."

"He won't have the chance," Gus said. "I'll kill you the instant you take your eyes off me."

"All right. I'll save you that. But—" She sobbed and her vocals clicked off.

"Let me explain further," it said. "You're wrong to see me as a monster, though I admit to having been partly at fault.

"I've never met another spacefaring race that believed itself to have individual consciousnesses. Individual wills for each part, certainly; otherwise it could hardly be mobile. I assumed . . .

"You see, sometimes my own parts wish to die in interesting ways. I approve; it adds to what I am. I assumed this is what you were doing. Nothing more."

"To business," Simmons said. "This is all very interesting. But immaterial, if you're just going to blow us to—"

"This was never the totality of my plan; for one thing, it will be a long time before you present any real threat to me, or to any other civilized race. I will not destroy you, not immediately."

"What do you mean by that?" Tshombe said.

Jacque's voice was getting weak; they strained to hear. "Consider me an observer, a monitor. A teacher, if you will learn."

"An executioner, if we won't," Svenbjørg said.

"Yes, but not in the sense of punishing you for wrongdoing." It paused. "I struggle with the limitations of your language, and with speaking through this one's pain.

"I have what you would call an obligation. To a sort of family, which includes organisms who would appear much stranger to you than I do—some of whom you wouldn't even recognize as life. And some so . . . sensitive that your mere presence would destroy them."

"You will guide us away from them?"

"Not necessary, yet. Those are still much too far away. Hopefully, by the time you can reach them, your own sensitivity will have evolved to where you are no longer a threat."

"If not, you'll warn us? Or them?"

"If not, I'll exterminate you. Which is the only way I can . . . legitimately interfere with your expansion. One day the logic of this will be clear to you."

"But what about the space we share?" Svenjbørg said. "Do we partition it? Share planets?"

"This is no real problem. You could not survive unprotected on worlds where I thrive. And I would stagnate on yours. I need

a great deal of hard radiation to properly reproduce my parts
—constant mutation and winnowing—that I may continue to
evolve at a proper rate. You reproduce too slowly to take advantage of this. Otherwise you might . . . We would have
to . . .

"This one dies. I sympathize with his pain. But his fear of
death amuses me. He—" A loud rattle choked off the last word.
The L'vrai released the bridge and Jacque's body pitched forward to the floor.

Carol spun and her laser glared green. The L'vrai's head
split at eye level and it toppled over, changing as it fell.

"Woman you might have—"

"Shut up!" Gus shouted. "She waited." Softer.

Carol glided to where her man lay and picked him up. She
stood immobile, silent.

Simmons approached her. "Woman? Listen to me. I used to
be a doctor. Let me see that man." Her crystal eyes stared down
at him.

"Ah, hell—" He grabbed Jacque's dangling arm and pulled.
Carol let go and he eased Jacque to the floor.

He ripped open Jacque's tunic and listened to his chest.
Then he straddled Jacque and started pounding on his sternum,
putting all his weight behind it.

"He's young . . . and healthy . . . get it . . . going here
. . ." The others gathered around, watching. He kept it up for
a while and put his ear down again.

"All right." He turned Jacque's head sideways, pinched
shut his nose, and began breathing into his mouth. In a few minutes, still unconscious, Jacque was breathing under his own
power.

Simmons sat back and panted. He glared up at Carol.
"Goddam it, don't just stand there. Get a real doctor."

GPEM suits are fast, but you have to watch out where you're
going. She narrowly missed trampling the Western Pope, and
widened their door by half a meter.

50
Mindbridge

Interspecies Communication With
the Groombridge Bridge: A Summary

1. Invertebrates

The most interesting invertebrate tested in conjunction with
the Groombridge bridge (also the first one) was another bridge.

Communicating with a bridge, via bridge, was not the immediate object of the experiment. The research team, in 2052,
was trying to enhance the Groombridge effect by using more
than one bridge per rapport-pair. If the two bridges touch, it
turns out, the effect is diminished, not increased (though if the
bridges are "in parallel"—one in each hand—the effect is the
same as with one bridge).

Some of the investigators reported vague feelings of "apprehension" or "uneasiness" when one bridge touched another,
though others reported no sensation. There was no apparent
correlation between this subjective response and the investiga-
tor's Rhine potential.

That the sensation is real was repeatedly verified by blind
testing: the two bridges connected by a conducting circuit that
could be opened and closed at random intervals by an unseen
observer.

This same apparatus was used in experiments with terrestrial animals. Only a few invertebrates (such as the tarantula
and the spiny lobster) produced repeatable responses. In no
case could experimenters identify the response with any discrete
human thought or emotion: in the words of one, it was "like the
feeling you might get when some barely audible sound stops.
You probably wouldn't notice it if you weren't concentrating."

2. Vertebrates

All vertebrates give some response; with few exceptions, the strength and complexity of the response is a direct function of brain size. Best results, predictably, came from experiments with simians and cetaceans.

(One researcher, Robert Graham of Charleville, claimed to have established communication on a verbal, conversational level with a pair of dolphins. His investigations have recently been discredited, as detailed in Section II.)

Section I following deals with the well-known perception and learning experiments conducted by Theodore Staupe of Colorado on chimpanzees and great apes. Section II details related work done with cetaceans by this author.

The response of other mammals is interesting but wildly variable, depending on the tester and the individual animal. Domesticated animals give the most complex responses; wild ones react mainly with fear. Section III following is a tabular assessment of all vertebrate data.

3. The L'vrai

A total of eleven people have attempted bridge rapport with th L'vrai. Four recorded no meaningful responses, but six suffered (apparently instantaneous) cardiac arrest. One died; the other five are now confined to mental institutions, mute and apparently oblivious to external stimuli. Autopsy revealed only a slight lesion on the rhinencephalon, which might have predated rapport.

Of course there is one individual, Jacque Lefavre, who has repeatedly communicated with the L'vrai via bridge rapport. His highly subjective account of the experience is appended in section VI following, through the courtesy of his publishers.

4. Apologia

Although this summary is profusely decorated with charts, graphs, statistics, and so forth, readers are warned to interpret our results with the skepticism they deserve. The data herein are for the most part subjective and nonrepeatable; where the data are quantified, the numbers are highly suspect. The summary is prepared in the spirit of a "state of the art" report, primarily to indicate directions for further research.

> Hugo Van der Walls, Ph.D.
> 14 July 2062
> AED Charleville

Contents:

51
Crystal Ball II

By 2090 people were getting nervous. Nobody but Jacque Lefavre had been able to maintain bridge rapport with the L'vrai, and Jacque was 75 years old. He probably had another quarter-century, but then what?

The L'vrai suggested a way that people could be tested for bridge potential without being turned into vegetables if they were unsuitable.

First, Lefavre was subjected to an exhaustive battery of psychological tests, that reduced his psyche to a computer full of numbers. People who roughly matched his profile were given the same battery of tests. The ones who came closest to "being" Lefavre were given a final test: sent to a remote corner of Groombridge, where the L'vrai waited. Isolated from the psychic pollution that random human sensibilities caused, the L'vrai didn't have to touch a candidate to tell whether he or she were suitable.

Candidate after candidate was rejected. Perhaps Jacque *was* unique. If so, humanity would be in a sorry state when he died— at the mercy of a creature whose nature was still a mystery, with whom communication was impossible. The L'vrai refused to read, write, or speak, claiming that expressing truth was impossible through the muddy filter of human language.

Jacque was 105, still hale, when his successor was found. Then two more, over the next few years.

A century later, there were several hundred who could communicate with the L'vrai; in a thousand years, every human could.

The L'vrai said it had not influenced human evolution directly; indeed, humans hadn't really changed in any basic way. They had only begun to see in their own nature the literal embodiment of *e pluribus unum* that described the L'vrai.

It withdrew its fleet from Sirius and allowed humankind the stars.

52
Autobiography 2149

(From *Peacemaker: The Diaries of Jacque Lefavre*, copyright © St. Martin's TFX 2151:)

EDITOR'S NOTE: Jacque Lefavre never made another entry in his diary after his beloved Carol died in 2112. But he continued service to humanity as emissary/translator to the L'vrai for another thirty years, until failing health forced him to retire.

The "ecstasy death" associated with primary contact in the Groombridge Effect had long been well-established. Lefavre desired it, and the AED was honored to comply.

They brought an untouched bridge to his bedside in upstate New York and, for his secondary contact, jumped in his great-granddaughter Tania Celarion. Of the twenty-eight great-grandchildren descended from the two children he and Carol had had, Tania was the one with the greatest Rhine potential, 458.

No meaningful number could be ascribed to Lefavre's potential, of course. Eighty years of association with the L'vrai had made him by far more sensitive than any other human being. He knew, therefore, that he wouldn't live long after he had touched the bridge.

In fact he lasted less than twenty seconds. But his great-granddaughter revealed in great detail, under contact hypnosis, what went through his mind in that short time.

Although this transcript has been reprinted often, it does seem a fitting way to end this collection.

I came in and sat down by his bed. He looked so old, I'd never seen anybody looked so old. I thought he was asleep but he wasn't. He just had trouble opening his eyes all the way. He smiled at me and said 'Tania, you make me wish I was a century younger," but the nurses told me he says that to any woman not in a wheelchair. And maybe he means it. He seems so good and pure, it's the Power he got from the Creepies, the L'vrai. It made him a little like a Creepy himself. He asked me how my mother was and all that relative drik, but I could see he couldn't keep his eyes off my box. The box I had the Groombridge Creepy in. Finally he asked me if we otta go ahead and do it, and I had to ask him did he really know he was going to die if he did? He said, "Child, I died thirty-seven years ago, and some months. Once I could tell you to the day, she was that much." Well, the nurses had warned me about that, too; all he ever talks about is my great-grandmother. Talked. Anyhow, he warned me not to touch the thing first, just open the box and let him touch it, and then get right in there with him because he didn't know how long it'd last.

Do you have that recorder on? Now most of this is what he said, but some of it's me bouncing off him. It's so important. You just listen and you can tell.

> There you are child. O your mind is so clean so new, may you never grow old and crowded. This is fun, I hope it doesn't give me a goddamn stroke; I've been inside woman's body Carol's, but never a little girl, so strange to feel the bones wanting to grow. You were little once too it's not so much fun when you're caught I know child in it, nothing ever fits once you get used to it I know I had a daughter why didn't you ever bridge *her* then. Well it seemed like a sexual thing and I guess it is but I don't really know what you're talking about but I don't feel shame, just that glow—say don't call me Jacque I'm as old as a goddamn planet call me Pop or Grandpop or I didn't call you Jacque or anything even, hey, you can't lie in bridge—there you did it again I DIDN'T CALL YOU NOTHING Jacque. No? . . . . I'm just a senile old fool Jacque I know that sound anywhere you have a special voice in bridge O shit it's sad to Jacque get so old you start Jacque kidding yourself Grandpop I hear it too don't humor me child angel bitch Jacque Jacque O God could they be right

Now I know that I'm just a little child and he was just an old man so nobody's gonna believe either of us. But I was there and I'll swear on anything you want that the voice was there, a woman's voice, soft, and if he said it was my great-grandmother then it was. Now I know you said that nobody else ever heard nothing like that but I don't care, *I* heard it, and if you don't want to believe me you can just go do yourself. Mom will believe me.

53
For They Shall
Be Called
the Children of God

In 2281 there was founded a planet (and splinter sect of Catholicism) named Nuovo Vaticano. They wanted to start their hagiographic calendar over clean: keeping such old saints as still had appeal, naming new ones as they saw fit.

The planet had to have a patron saint, and of course they didn't want it to be one of the old ones. Someone suggested Jacque Lefavre. All anybody knew was that he'd done good works in connection with the New Saviors, and that on his deathbed he'd offered some highly disputed proof of an afterlife.

Their small, practical library didn't have a copy of *Peacemaker*, so they had one sent on the next jump.

After reading the book thoroughly they decided Lefavre would be a bad example for their children.